<u>The Locket</u>

a novel by Marianne Puechl

Jemima Creek Signature Books

Asheville, NC

Please visit the author's website for additional works,
contact information & links to social media:

www.MariannePuechl.com

©2013 Jemima Creek Signature Books
a division of Artistic Ventures, Inc. / Asheville, NC / USA

Cover Design by M. Puechl & Ira Adams
Title font created by Hannah Marlin

ISBN 978-0-9726892-0-5

Artistic Ventures, Inc.
PO Box 17596
Asheville, NC 28816
(828) 645-8750

for Cindy & for Kestin
...and all those who choose to perceive the extraordinary

The Locket

Chapter One

There was a bite to the air outside, but inside with the thick sprigs of ivy and the candlelit lanterns, the laughter and the oily smell of sweet baked cheese, a warmth had risen and held on. The flow of chianti warmed too, belly-outwards, and the conversations all around: people conjuring life together.

It was her birthday. She sat off to the corner, but not alone. The friend with her was of obvious high spirits, and of a brightness like wild colors and the kind of laughter that ripples waves wall to wall.

She was revealed when the little Italian waiter came by, presenting the white wedge of cake and cream, and when the man with the violin stopped to offer serenade. It was her birthday, and though she didn't quite notice, it was true she felt happy tonight.

They bundled themselves as they left, leaving the ambiance of the restaurant for the chilly midautumn night air. The sidewalk was wet with an earlier rain; it glistened and blinked with the lights of the district. The women huddled close, still giggling. It was as if the snap of the cold and outdoors helped them feel the earlier sense of warmth all the more keenly.

"You went overboard, Greta. And I thank you!"

Greta smiled, but then winked and fell to smugness. "Oh we're not done yet. Here-" And abruptly she tugged her friend into a small doorway. The entry opened into a wall of scarves, scattered reds and oranges and a flurry of patterns making way as the women entered through. Within, a sitting room of fine décor. Three china teacups waited on the little table.

Greta offered the same look of smugness and pulled off her coat. "Come sit at the table, Bee. She'll be out in a minute."

"And who are we talking about?" Bee did not remove her coat. A smell of incense wafted past; it brought her to wonder.

But Greta would not answer. She took a seat, bit her lip with obviousness, and fell to silence. Bee eyed the room again, studying the thick drawn curtains and the Victorian wallpaper; the tiny receiving bench and the lace cloth on the table. Not long and a little woman entered from the room beyond. Bee faced her skeptically.

She had a big nose, and thin crescent eyes that were dark and unreadable. With the stature of an old woman, she scuffed her heels across the wooden floor and to the worn Oriental rug... yet she was obviously no more than fifty. Around the thinness of her neck hung a long chain of gold and she wore an emerald nugget on her finger, and it seemed doubtful she would do anything other than sit right down, sharply utter a few sparse words and things would suddenly begin between them all, but instead the little woman walked to Bee and extended a gracious hand.

"Hello, so nice to meet you," she smiled, her dark eyes kind somehow. "Please come sit at my table, I have tea waiting. I am absolutely certain that Miss Greta told you nothing of this…" And she rolled her eyes and smiled to Greta. "She wanted to be sure to surprise you."

"Oh no need to be discreet," Greta crooned, swatting at the air. "Bee knows full well that I had to trick her to get her within a mile of something like this. Now sit down, and take your medicine. Your birthday, I get to give you the gift I damn well want to!" And she laughed, gesturing to an empty chair.

The older woman sat down first, then Bee followed. Finally, she took off her coat.

"My name is Catherine," said their hostess, pouring tea. "Greta asked for my services, because she thought it fitting for the anniversary of your birth. I'm a psychic of course, but you already knew that." She grinned, and took a moment to watch Bee's expression. "Now don't worry over the tea, Darling, it's just chamomile and mint. A little something for relaxing, that's all. No potions, I assure you."

Bee gave a hard glance to Greta. "Remember what I said outside?" She feigned a grumble. "Forget it. And by the way, you're fired."

Greta patted her hand and asked Catherine to begin. "I for one can't stand to wait another minute for this!"

The psychic cleared her throat. A handful of playing cards appeared, worn and thin. Catherine asked Bee to pick several, and she set them out on the lace cloth. -Jack of clubs, Queen of spades… Five of spades, Ace of diamonds… Five of diamonds, the Joker…

Catherine did not pause for dramatics, nor did she speak mysteriously.

3

She simply put, "Well, no hearts speaks of something of course. A lot of spades yet, and the Ace of diamonds. I can tell professionally you are very successful; a high achiever and well-liked. You have a choice to make every day although you are unaware of it- you can stay on the track and become even more successful, or you can choose another way and learn of different things. But success will always meet you when it comes to your business life."

Greta nodded in strong agreement. Bee kept still.

"Of course you have a little child. She is an angel to you; a kind of balance if you will. It is a blessing that she is in your life."

This brought even Bee to a smile. Greta nodded again, this time beaming. "Molly is fantastic."

The psychic continued. "There is a pull, with another female in your family life. This has a darkness to it; a foggy sort of darkness. Perhaps it is with someone who has passed on?"

Bee did not respond. She only reached for her tea.

"There are men of wealth around you, men of all kinds, but none close. This is as it should be right now." Catherine paused a moment. Then she looked up across the table. "What is your full name, my Dear?"

"Oh, everyone calls me Bee."

"Yes," she said, politely. But her eyes now were a hard focus.

Bee breathed deep, took another sip of tea. "Abbey Elana Taft."

Greta smiled again and whispered, "It is so pretty…"

Catherine agreed. "It is a beautiful name. Now," and she drew another card from the deck, the nine of hearts. "Yes. You do know that there is a piano waiting for you. It is silent, but it waits."

Bee grimaced. "Well I'm not much of a player, really."

"Mm." Catherine paused, again her eyes were hard. Then she smiled sincerely, as if to the wisdom in Bee's own gaze. "The playing isn't really the issue, of course." And she went on, "You'll want to break through some of this fog, Abbey, so that it doesn't descend unto your daughter as well. These things truly can be passed down. Usually they are, as a matter of course. You won't want that to happen again."

Greta watched, intrigued, as something of the look on Bee's face wore to a stoic tightness. Something of a knot pulling in on itself, and then not moving.

Catherine, in her lovely hand-sewn, beaded dress and with the even tone of her voice, suddenly seemed a contrast to herself. There was a sure edge to what she was saying, though the words were lyrical, and they drifted somehow softly out into the corners of the room.

"...and up that hill you'll find... ...when your father was alive... ...it has to do with that ingrained idea you have about... ...when your boss deals with it... ...like the sky, as it changes from clear to cloudy, and back again... ...and back again... ...a little hint of jewelry, perhaps from her but perhaps not at all from her, perhaps with a little neckchain... ...it may be symbolic of the movement away from this idea with her/movement to-ward this new idea with her... ...with the winds shifting... ...and back again. And back again. And back again."

It was her birthday. Suddenly, that was what crossed her mind. It was a thought that nestled and hung midair, caught all her focus, and anchored her. She was grateful for it really, and it cut off the drone of all else. Forty-two years old... Forty-two years young... Forty-two years old... Forty-two years young... And she realized she was sitting off to the corner. But not alone.

"...Well go ahead, Bee," Greta was saying. She gripped Abbey's hand and tugged at her. "Go ahead and pick the last card."

Bee came to, facing the women across the table and smiling a bit in pretending that she had been listening all along. She mentioned flippantly that there was a grey spider up in the corner of the Victorian wallpaper, crossing to the drapes. Catherine did not look away, but fanned the deck of cards and only nodded politely.

With a quick motion, Bee grabbed a card, and set it down. The Ace of Hearts.

"Hell yeah!" Greta boomed. Catherine brightened too.

"Yes, yes, there you are then. Let me just say... At your next estate sale, it's true that you'll find something. You'll forget about it, but you'll remember again. It's important. Something to do with your-" And she reached and patted Bee sweetly. "-with your quest, about the search for love. -Truelove."

Then there was a shuffle of goodbyes, donning of coats, a few thank-you's and Bee and Greta were outside again, snapped into the cold. Bee gulped in the air, welcoming it so, this time for the coldness that it was; not for the warmth it helped define. "It's familiar," she said to Greta, who pummeled her with sudden questions. "Familiar, Greta. Yes, I suppose it feels good."

Greta Duvall was a middle-aged black woman, a brilliant spirit who had a master's degree in classical philosophy, had been a professor, a short-order cook, a social worker, a newspaper editor, a housekeeper, of course a taxi cab driver and even one season had been the caretaker of a lighthouse somewhere and heroically saved the life of a fisherman during a midwinter storm. She was impeccably dependable and had the forethought of a gypsy; the humor of a good bartender; the eyes of a hawk. She had the capability of being a menacing woman indeed, but with the kind of full and compassionate heart that made her a poet as well. Abbey knew all of these things, and felt it one of the luckiest points of her life to have employed Greta as nanny to her four-year-old daughter.

As she lay awake in the darkness before dawn, Bee let her thoughts wander to the circumstances of Greta and her brilliance; of the way this woman lived and shared her life. And she thought of her daughter, Molly, and the wonders the little girl was learning from her time with Greta, and the beauty that it was.

And she thought of her work… her recent projects and her upcoming ones. And that was all. She did not think of the fog outside, rolling away with the coming of dawn. She did not think of it, but watched abstractly as the darkness gave way to mild orange, then lightness outright. And she rose from bed and made coffee.

Chapter Two

The heat of the coffee stung at her lips this morning, then slowly made its way down; it reminded Bee of the night before. She snickered a little, sat at the high island in the middle of the kitchen, and opened her newspaper.

The kitchen itself was a perfect size: plenty of working room, counterspace and cabinets. The only drawback was the lighting here, according to Greta. The two windows and the indirect light from the open dining area beyond simply could not contend with the dark oaken cabinets and the low ceiling.

On one counter was a small television set, and when little Molly padded sleepily into the room, Bee switched on the remote control. Quietly, the buzz of cartoons filled the corners of the kitchen. Bee lifted Molly onto her lap, kissed her good morning and asked how she'd slept.

"Mommy had a nice time out to dinner. A man played me a birthday song on his violin and they gave me a big piece of cake with creamy white icing and yellow flowers on it."

Molly muttered a question.

"Mmm… it was a white cake with a little bit of raspberry in it too." Bee squeezed the girl, waking her more. "How was your babysitter?"

Molly nodded and said, "Good," then fell to watching the cartoons. After just a brief moment she added details about playing hide 'n' seek, setting up the train track, and making popcorn. Bee gave her another kiss then spread open her paper again, well-practiced in her Saturday lean so that Molly could watch the cartoons.

"How old are you, Mommy?" piped the little voice, some time later. It brought a splash of textured Victorian red to Abbey's mind. And suddenly there was a knock at the back door.

Molly squealed gleefully as Greta peeked her head in and entered with a grin. Jumping down, the child raced for a hug. Abbey only stared at her paper. "It's Saturday," she said suspiciously, "Mary Poppins…"

Greta ignored her, instead helping Molly to pick out some cereal. She poured juice, taking her time, and wondered aloud, "So who wants to go shopping today? You can't beat 3 girls shopping on a Sat-ur-day!"

The four-year-old shrieked an echo.

The Victorian red flashed like a sudden flare, though it was fleeting. "Does it count as real 'karma'?" Abbey asked, raising a playful brow, "when you plan it out like this?"

Greta maintained her expression, passing a glass of juice. Dryly she replied, "Hey. Karma is karma."

The cartoon was a good one. Greta and Molly watched awhile. When the cereal was gone, the woman winked to the little girl and urged her over. As she retrieved a hairband and brush from one of the drawers,

Greta whispered to her: "We gotta hurry, Miss Molly. And you gotta help me get Mommy excited."

"Yeah…" She thought a moment, then blurted, "Oh it'll be the funnest day, Mommy!"

Bee couldn't help but smile across to the pair of them, brightening as she watched their enthusiasm.

Of course Greta offered to drive, and it wasn't long before they were following signs across town. Molly practiced reading her letters "S-A-L-E" and pointed the way turn after turn. Once out of the car the girl hurried ahead, quickly spotting a row of colored dresses and a jumble of shoes on display.

Abbey and Greta lagged behind. "You know, she talked like I regularly go to these things. I mean, I haven't been to an estate sale since my dad took me. I was maybe twelve or something."

"Well I don't know why she mentioned Truelove either," Greta gibed. "We just need to get you laid, that's all really."

Bee exaggerated a look of shock, then chuckled. "Sure, I guess that would be… ah-hmm… nice. -The best of both worlds, maybe."

Greta moved ahead, entering the house. Molly sat wide-legged on the porch steps, trying on ladies shoes one after the other. Miscellaneous housewares lined the first tables, then some faux jewelry. Bee fingered a strand of beads for Molly's dress-up, then reconsidered. Instead, she picked out a tiny purse and a scarf.

Then she took Molly's hand, leading her inside where they eyed furniture, lamps, blankets and a corner full of old tools. They came upon a table of old toys, some antique, and Abbey spent time showing her daughter the little porcelain figures, the mechanical coin bank, wooden tops and a pair of toy binoculars.

Molly noticed the delicate care of her mother's gaze over the toys, and further along to the little sewing kit and hand-crocheted shawls… She watched as Bee leafed through thinning pages of paper, then the little girl sneezed at the smell of dust and wandered off to find Greta.

Abbey lingered, the feel of the worn pages of sheet music tender between her hands. -These were the elements of her own parents' world, of her mother's house and home… To see and feel them suddenly brought a haze over her eyes: Bee stashed a few pages under her arm and moved away.

She went back to the toys and directly picked up the coin bank, then surveyed the room for Greta and Molly. They were heading back around to the front door. Shrugging herself into a broad grin, Abbey joined them, oohing and ahhing over the pink shoes Molly had finally decided upon. Greta was empty-handed and, noticeably, kept quiet as she looked over Abbey's choices. Abbey glanced to her wryly, but Greta only smiled softly and moved ahead.

There was a line for making payment. Abbey waited stoically, then let her mind wander a bit to the late owners of this house; the things they'd collected then left behind. It was not a happy line of thought, and an obscure part of her wondered why such ponderings were so typically and decidedly somber. Couldn't there be some way to turn it all around? Couldn't some part of this inevitable process be gleaned in a different light?

The oddity of the lingering thoughts jarred her. In an abrupt motion, the woman turned and looked out into the backyard, out and away.

…And something there caught all her attention.

"Can I help you, Ma'am?" -The estate attendant's voice was calling to her. "Are you ready with your purchase?"

Abbey only shook her head, and made her way out toward the green of the yard through the open back door. The wind was light, and it soothed her; drew her along even more completely.

Outside over the open-air porch hung a menagerie of hand-fashioned birdhouses: little shacks, little steeples; dried gourds, tiny pebbled landscapes; old cedar, pinecone shingles… And there, hanging midst that quaint miniature neighborhood, was an ugly strand of fishing line knotted with jumbled old keys. It was several strands of line, actually, almost like a mobile with keys hanging at different lengths so that with the fresh wind they clinked together in a worn and heavy harmony. Many of the keys were rusted, and the spindle at the top that held the thing together was a threesome of bent forks.

"Well this is as rustic as it can be," Abbey said aloud, barely noticing the perfect yellow trim on the birdhouse just alongside. And she pulled the keys down, and headed back to wait in line.

———————————————

Not long and they arrived back home, Molly racing up the steps to gather a dress-up outfit from her room to match the new pink shoes.

Bee set her things down on the kitchen counter, shrugging a breath as she decided on lunch. Greta smiled to her and patted her arm. "Well *I* have a date tonight, so I'm going to head on."

Eyeing her fixed expression, Abbey put to her, "You're still being mysterious, aren't you?"

"Call it what you will, I guess," the woman said, refraining from any show of smugness. Instead she patted Bee again, saying sincerely, "Happy, happy birthday Bee."

As she left, Bee paused to look over her collection of wares: a few pages of sheet music, the old coin bank, a purse and scarf for Molly, the jumble of keys and a large scuffed cigar box. "...Treasures all," she muttered, mimicking a saying of her father's. -Strange, she realized, how he kept popping into her thoughts today.

Taking a longer moment, she ran fingers around the old cigar box, lifted it and sniffed for a hint of its odor: heavy, musty, just a subtle implication of its original use... mostly the thick smell of time passed -the passage of time- and a mix of the sweet perfumed scent that had permeated the couple's home. Funny how all that could be packed into a little moment; a quick sniff of ancient pressboard... It brought a smile to Abbey, the kind of smile that nourished and warmed and saddened, and it reassured her somehow.

"A day for chicken soup," she said aloud, mocking herself for getting so nostalgic. The loud clang of the pot and whir of the can opener helped revive her; she set the soup on simmer and wandered out to the dining room and up the stairs.

Abbey and Molly's house was well-organized, trimmed with tasteful furniture and simple colors. There was very little to catch an eye or pose a surprise -everything was in its place, and predictably so. Beiges, light blue, bright white chair moulding and quiet wallpapers with tiny flowers and stripes. Tasteful, organized, comfortable. A little sterile, perhaps. But familiar.

The most extreme was the deep burgundy, textured wallpaper in the dining room. It was utterly formal, and Bee's furniture was a complement, but it was too extreme to match the rest of the house. Ultimately Abbey said she hoped to tone it down to a charming cream print, perhaps retain the burgundy with new drapes and maybe the artwork to coincide. 'Burgundy,' Greta had said many times, 'a good color for dining.'

Upstairs was the master bedroom and bath, along with a guest room and Molly's bedroom. The four-year-old stooped in her doorway as Abbey climbed the stairs. The little girl was tugging on a pair of white tights, her wide brimmed straw hat slipping with every motion. Bee watched her a while, then leaned in to help and to add the final touches with the new scarf and purse.

Together, they ventured to the mirror. Molly squealed. Abbey squeezed her gleefully and smacked a kiss on her cheek.

"You want to go see Grandma today, and show her your pink shoes, and bring her a bunch of pretty balloons for Mommy's birthday?"

Molly squealed again, and kissed her mother in return.

Chapter Three

"Bonaday's Care Home" read the sign out front of the length of bricks & shutters, the sidewalks and porches. It was a large facility, but had some charm. It was nestled off a quiet cul-de-sac, the property included two acres filled with trees, several open grassy areas, picnic benches, walkways and a small pond. The residents' rooms looked out over the grounds, most faced the landscaped courtyard in the middle of the building. Abbey felt relieved at having found such a pleasant and inviting place for her mother's final years. It was a place of life; not of waiting or wanting, desperation or simply dying. It was a home.

And Abbey and Molly visited frequently, though the visits themselves weren't always quite so peaceful as it seemed they should be. And that contradiction made things hard sometimes, in a twist of emotions too subtle and too jagged to name.

Today Molly paraded into the community room with a bouquet of balloons, pinks and yellows, purples and silver. Most everyone took notice of her ear-to-ear grin and her billowing colors... Missy Hendricks and John-Wyatt, eyes up from their board game, had to urge

Caroline Taft to glance up too and watch.

"Hi Mom," Abbey smiled, but Caroline kept her gaze now on the motion of the balloons. "Hello Missy, hello John-Wyatt…"

The two smiled to Abbey and across to the little girl. "Your Molly sure looks proud," Missy said, then turned to Caroline and took on a sharper tone. "That's *your* Molly, Caroline. And here's Abbey too… Caroline? You behave yourself today! Mind your manners."

Abbey leaned in to kiss her mother's cheek, winking across the table in thanks to Missy.

"Look, Grammy!" Molly finally said, marching closer to the group of them. The balloons bounced in Caroline's face; with a grimace she knocked them aside.

Abbey stretched and tugged the balloons away, reminding the little girl to give her grandma a kiss. She did so, and Caroline met her gaze.

"Oh," Missy interjected, "how your grandma does love you, Molly."

Abbey handed back the balloons. "Here Sweetie, stand back a little bit and you can march all around the table. Grammy will like watching the colors." After a moment, Bee reached across the table for her mother's hand. "It's my birthday today, remember Mom?"

"Oh how special," said Missy.

John-Wyatt passed a tin of cookies. "Oatmeal raisin," he offered. "Betsy made them. She makes good cookies, I must say."

Abbey thanked him, though abruptly Caroline interrupted and roughly grabbed for the tin. She snatched a cookie and chewed quickly. "Betsy makes good cookies," she spoke finally. "Oatmeal, isn't it? With the raisins?"

Missy rolled her eyes at Caroline's tone. Bee asked, "Mom, can I have a cookie too?"

Caroline watched her somewhat suspiciously, slow to hand over the tin. Abbey waited patiently, then added, "I'm your little girl, remember? Like John-Wyatt has Betsy, you have me. You had Kate and then me, and then Cale. Three children." She paused, watched her mother. The woman only blinked. "My name is Bee, I'm Molly's mommy."

With that Caroline glanced to the dancing balloons, then agreed to pass the cookies.

Missy called the little girl over to join them, tied up the balloons onto her chair and settled her in with a cookie. Abbey commented about Betsy's recipe, adding, "I'm forty-two today, John-Wyatt. Do you have any advice for me?"

"At forty-two? Hell, no. Just have a good time, Darlin. Don't worry about it. Come ask me again in thirty years. Until then, just have a good time."

Caroline pointed a stiff finger toward the birthday girl, wrenching her lips into a stern expression. "Eat your vitamins."

"Well," Missy giggled, "that's not bad advice either, eh?"

Abbey managed a smile, and patted John-Wyatt gratefully. "I'll try to take your words to heart too, John-Wyatt. Though it's easy to forget, at forty-two, that I'm still-"

"*Young*," he grinned to her. "You are young, My Dear. And all is well. That's pretty much all there is to it. Don't complicate things for yourself."

They all sat quietly awhile, munching cookies. Then Missy asked

Molly how her friends were doing. "Good," piped the youngster.

"And what do you like to play with your friends?"

"School… And Princess Dress-Up!" At once, she pulled her new pink shoes from her backpack and handed them around the table. Abbey chuckled at her, then let her attention drift from the little girl back to her mother. The older woman was staring out away from the table, toward the sunshine in the far windows.

'…when Betsy was little, she loved to play dress-up. She'd get into her mother's jewelry box and make a mess of all the necklaces. I remember my wife howling over that time and time again… Now don't you go into your mama's jewelry, Molly, unless she says it's all right. You hear?'

Abbey focused hard on the sunlight too, trying to glean from it a whisper or two of the wonders it held for her mother. Lilting sparkles on the pane of glass… a prism of color and then briefly again… simple brightness… there, and not here…

'…well when I was a little girl I loved to climb trees and go ice skating, and in the summer go swimming in the pond. We'd catch frogs too, and watch the tadpoles grow all spring long. We didn't have lots of clothes for dress-up…'

There, and not here… Somewhat dazedly, Bee pulled at the backpack and retrieved the old sheet music she'd bought at the estate sale. She stood and quietly showed it to her mother.

"Look what I found, Mom. Do you remember how you loved 'Satin Doll?' And look, some Scott Joplin."

Missy watched them together, then suggested, "You know Bee, why don't you take your mom for a little walk? She likes to get around."

Abbey agreed and helped her mother up. The older woman leaned toward the bright windows, but instead Bee nudged her toward the organ. The two sat together on the bench, Abbey set up the sheet music, turned on the organ and began to play the left-hand part of a Joplin rag.

Caroline smiled lightly at the sound, and watched as Bee's fingers danced across the lower keyboard. Others around the room too were delighted at the music.

Her mother's fingers were stiff with reluctance, but Abbey positioned them over the keys just so, to join in the melody line. Then in a lively but even tempo, Bee re-played the Joplin. Over and over, she repeated the passage… and smiled to urge her mother on.

Eventually Caroline banged down on the keys completely out of tempo. She did try again, but the sounds frightened her. Abbey picked up the melody and finished out the phrase, and when she sat back the room came alive with gentle clapping.

Bee stared at the woman, who faced her awhile although the look in her eyes seemed rather blank. Abbey began to speak, a little teary, then decided against it. Once again in silence, they remained there at the organ bench for some time.

A nurse wandered by with a tray, smiled and invited them back to the table for lemonade. Caroline perked an eager grin and Abbey paused, hopeful that her mother might turn to her and share the moment -ask for some help returning to the table- but instead Caroline only slid herself down off the organ bench and began shuffling across the linoleum. Abbey followed, took another deep breath and steadied herself.

"MMmmm, lemonade!" Molly piped, pursing her lips with the tartness. Missy and John-Wyatt beamed at the girl, then said their goodbyes and left the family to their visit.

Again, Abbey sat in silence for a time and the three sipped at their lemonade. Molly tugged a little doll free from her backpack and offered the toy a bit of leftover oatmeal cookie. The sunlight in from the windows waned just a bit.

Abruptly Caroline's voice broke the quiet: "Balloons are nice. Tea parties are nice, too."

Molly grinned to her grandma, who was suddenly alive with movement. Her hands were unsteady but quick, and all at once the glasses and napkins and pitcher were set just so about the table.

"Tea parties are nice…" the old woman repeated. She drew back the pitcher to pour, but only a few drops were left.

Molly didn't mind, and encouraged her grandma to keep pouring. Abbey watched on, fascinated by the connection between her mother and her daughter, with a twinge in her heart at the sight.

Yet the moment wasn't long -Caroline had grown frustrated by the empty pitcher. She sat and stared hard at the table, in obvious thought, then a brow quivered and she reached out toward the sheet music there beside Abbey.

Her fingers had changed so much, Bee noticed, remembering the mother who had helped her learn to tie shoes; the mother who had shown her first notes on the piano; braided her hair; flipped through pages of term papers; beckoned her with a point and a turn of that hand to pay closer attention and comply…

Now these fingers were grey somehow, with less pink and tone to them. They were swollen in new places and the nails were unpainted. But they were still soft, Abbey knew, uncalloused and alive with the beat that was somehow her mother.

Caroline tugged at the sheet music, never facing Bee's gaze. And methodically, without a pause, the old woman began tearing the pages into little shreds and dropping them into the empty glasses.

"Tea parties are nice," she said once again, and raised a glass with Molly so they could pretend to drink.

Chapter Four

Abbey Taft had begun her professional life in a small branch of an insurance company, quickly moved into underwriting and worked there diligently as she completed her MBA. After graduate school, her resume circulating, she took a position at Hyer's Bank in Minneapolis. It was there she spent her late twenties and thirties. Life seemed to revolve around a select few things: her career, several evenings a week joining in the nightlife and spending time with friends, her brisk and exotic vacation getaways, keeping her parents and most other family members at a comfortable distance, sidestepping the dry monotony of settling down.

Later, though not unexpectedly, the atmosphere at the bank did nothing but turn in on itself and grow more and more stale. Bee came to find that, although she herself enjoyed promotion after promotion, and generous benefits and compensation for her seniority at Hyer's, that time and again in her managerial role she was forced to sit down with staff members and try to explain why they, on the other hand, could expect no promotion and certainly no raise.

Abbey tried moving laterally -when Hyer's merged with a large national bank she made her way out of the weather of Minneapolis and into an office in Manhattan… but the change didn't change enough. Suddenly however Abbey was pregnant, so she remained at the bank a bit longer. Molly's arrival was another clear reason to leave the long hours and hectic pace of NYC; shortly after the baby's first birthday Abbey took a new job indeed: senior editor for *Mosaic* Women's Magazine.

She and Molly moved to New Jersey, the hustle and staleness gave way to fresh scenery. The job was quite a difference for Bee, but the magazine had been in dire need of a strong supervisor to oversee several departments, and Abbey was ready for a new feel to her life.

Work as a senior editor was certainly well-paced, but some of the dryness was gone. And the new slant of creativity so potent in the office everyday was nothing less than revitalizing.

Abbey had settled in. Quickly, with pride in herself for making the switch and for doing it her own way. Happily too, in that it felt right for her and Molly to begin building a niche for themselves in this quiet rural township.

Today, she bustled into the office, said a few quick words to her assistant and concentrated fully on the schedule of the day. A busy series of month-end meetings claimed her Monday. Bee dabbed at her lipstick, grabbed her coffee and hustled back through the building toward the conference room.

It was a daunting task, overseeing the wild array of deadlines and organizational details, piecing together those disjointed fragments into a national magazine. Abbey was not in charge of layout, or the ever-changing list of advertisers, she did not handle the graphics or photo assignments. Nonetheless she remained aware of all those aspects of the upcoming issues, as well as keenly involved with her own direct responsibilities. "It's like being a surgeon," Bee had been told once and now repeated to her staff. "And for some reason this month -maybe it's just Halloween- there's an air of mischief to it all; but we'll manage just fine. Steady hands, steady heads, Everybody."

"So now Sam, did that interview with the mayor stay on course?"

Sam Beauregard, political and special events editor, offered a solid nod. His words came fast. "Not a hitch. Well-focused with just a few digressions. All good personable moments though, so I kept them. Sharp with the environmental concerns and the park and greenspace funding. I like Julie: she interviews well." He smiled and dropped a page of spec/s before Abbey. "Who knows? Maybe I'll vote for her this year…"

Another editor spoke in turn, "Stories Four, Five and Six are all completed as well, nothing out of sync to discuss. Word counts are right on. 225: celebrity hot picks, 987: health, 1550: celebrity interview."

Others echoed similar details. This particular issue was a more complicated layout design, but things were pulling together. There was no reason to foresee a problem, but Abbey stayed watchful: something unusual buzzed about in the air. There was an unsettled feeling; an uncertainty that lingered since her evening with the psychic.

Later, back in her office just before lunchtime, an email came through from Bee's supervisor -sure enough, it did not bode well. And something about it, as she read it through, brought words from Catherine to mind: 'You have a choice to make every day professionally although you're unaware of it...' And Abbey breathed a deep exhale, remembering.

Trouble with the report from D.C. I've been unable
to corroborate the last references about the evolution
of the new anti-abortion question and the comments
from the Senator. Check into it, not only with Sam
but with Ben Cole -
let's get some objectivity and FIND OUT
WHAT IS GOING ON.

Edward L. Endeen, vice president
Mosaic Magazine

Abbey exhaled again, then gathered herself and called her assistant. "I'll need some take-out Robin," she said. "And call Sam for me. Squeeze him in for a meeting at 1:20."

_____

Ben Cole was one of the freelance writers *Mosaic* contracted on occasion. He was articulate, intelligent, ambitious and certainly well-connected: this was the strong point in which Abbey's VP was most interested. At least currently. Ben was also a nice guy, everyone said. But Abbey tried to keep her distance. Yet tonight she had no choice.

"Good to see you, Abbey," he said, grinning warmly and reaching for her hand.

Abbey shook formally then stepped ahead toward the table. "Emergency drinks," she said, attempting a smile. "Thank you for meeting on such short notice."

"Ah well," and he toasted her. "My pleasure."

The waiter stopped by and Bee ordered a gin and tonic. Then she stated without further pause, "I've got a situation. Some of the political stories are coming through with major inaccuracies-"

"Ah-hmmmm." He interrupted her flatly. And Bee noticed for the first time how the deep brown of his eyes was somehow… captivating.

She blinked, then met his gaze again with a reconsidered focus, hopeful he hadn't noticed the break.

"I was thinking maybe we could ease into this," Ben said. "-Enjoy ourselves a little, despite the work. You know." And he let go of the stare, glancing around at the strands of lights and the rustic hues of the bar.

Abbey wondered a moment, sipped at her gin and called him back. "Well as you know, I have a daughter to get home to. And two more early meetings tomorrow to prepare for."

He paused. "I know about your daughter. She's… five?"

"Four and a quarter. -The quarter's very important." And she allowed a shared smile. "You don't have kids, do you?"

He shook his head. "Never married."

"Me neither." And she thought how to turn things back around. She wished she might just bluntly put to him: 'You know Ben, I'm technically your boss when we hire you to write for us…' But somehow this man seemed more like her rival, and feeling so awkward was a strange sensation indeed for Abbey Taft. Must be that hint of last Friday's uncertainty again, or the changing seasons, she thought, nudging things off-balance.

"What was that?" Ben asked.

"Oh," she said, not realizing she had muttered a few words. Quickly she added, "Well I wondered what you were working on now?" And she raised her glass again, vowing that this sip would prove to be the one to finally settle her.

The writer went on about a project or two, including some surprisingly interesting details about a travel book he was partnering on. But as his words ebbed, Abbey started right in with the work before them, here with *Mosaic*. And fifteen minutes later she made her way back out of the bar.

"So there's somebody lying, that's the bottom line," Greta observed, munching a cracker as she sat with Abbey tonight in the living room.

"Yep. Misquoting senators can get us into some trouble." Bee shrugged. "I'll try a couple more things tomorrow, but there's a good chance I'll have to fly to Washington later this week."

Greta nodded.

"Not a fun part of the job, I must say. But… I'll book myself a nice hotel, that'll be something."

"Oh you like traveling, Bee," Greta said knowingly, eyeing her as the woman reached for the box of crackers. "Dinner?" she chided. "See? You like being on the go."

"Well, sometimes," Abbey said. And she rose to check in on Molly as the nanny gathered herself to leave for the night. "Thanks, Greta."

Molly was sound asleep, the thin loose curls of her hair a dark frame behind the silhouette of her little nose and chin. Her mother crept in quietly, careful not to bump the several mobiles hanging from the ceiling. 'Molly is always looking up,' Greta had often said. 'It's a gift that ought to be encouraged.'

A white dress-up outfit, hat and the pink shoes were all clinging to the rocking chair near the bed. Abbey lifted them aside and sat to rock, eyes on the tender sleep of her four-year-old. 'I barely remember four,' she thought to herself. And the vision of her daughter, back at Bonaday's, came to mind: balloons sailing, knees up for the march… It brought Bee to a smile. 'Four is a time to be silly and bright and…'

"Molly, you're perfect," she said aloud. And she rocked some more, gently, realizing just how content it made her feel to be here.

Chapter Five

It was true, Abbey Taft liked looking the part. -She'd seen it just now, reflected in the concierge's glance, and it reconnected her somehow back into herself. It brought a quick memory to mind of a girlhood toy -a flimsy little ragdoll- and how time and time again her mother would sew an arm or button eye back in place. Something of the memory jostled her; Abbey focused back onto the twist of her heel and the sway of her hip as she approached the elevator.

The hotel room was immaculate. :Well-stocked bar, hot tub, bath salts, European candies on the pillow. It had been a good decision to pamper herself. -Resolving matters here in D.C. was not going to be easy. At least the nights would be.

Abbey's first day in the city began like details from a restless dream. The hours were chopped; snapshot interactions that cut and severed themselves. Early coffee and sharp words with one of their D.C. journalists… an opportune but rather bewildering 5 minutes with an assistant of the Senator's… a shared cab with an opinionated circuit judge… a pretzel with mustard up by the Mall and a solid moment's conversation with a lone tourist from Ireland.

The afternoon went surprisingly well, however: another tense but productive phone call with the journalist and doors suddenly opening to the Senator's office… All at once one major issue was solved. Abbey thought to attribute the run of luck to nothing other than her visit with the Irishman: something of a little leprechaun elf must be at the heart of it, she mused. Perhaps there was no Halloween black mischief to worry over after all; indeed maybe for her this was all a sign of *good* fortune.

And secretly she smiled. Greta herself would be proud of such musings.

That night when the concierge stared in her direction Abbey knew it was more than the strong-willed, fit business professional that caught his attention. Tonight it was the lively beauty of a confident woman, sharp-eyed and bright, who knew well she'd worked a successful business day. And she felt sexy, as well as single, and above all else luck had proven its new loyalty… Bee grinned and entered the cab that had been hailed for her.

She had turned down a dinner offer from one of the *Mosaic* affiliates and instead headed unaccompanied out to Georgetown. A little club she'd seen in the paper had struck her: *Baited Jazz*.

Bee sat at a small table, ordered an appetizer, and sat back to watch the momentum throughout the room. No one ventured over, but it didn't surprise her. At the moment, she felt like savoring the perspective of the onlooker. Inevitably, she knew, it would lead to something.

Sure enough, once the appetizer was gone, an approach presented itself. Two, in fact. There was a man at the bar who seemed interesting enough; he'd been making conversation with a couple for a little while but now he was by himself, ear to the piano and sax off in the far corner. And further along, past the turn of the counter, sat a lone young woman, designer suit layered over her torso like a perfect rendering. Everything about the way the light played about her seemed to dart away sure focus, and make the lilt of the saxophone drone into a lower, deeper, pulsed vibration. Abbey took her wine glass and strode toward the bar. Rounding just past its oaken middlepoint, she slid next to the woman and asked, "Do I know you?" -A flirtatious inflection so she'd get the right idea from the start.

The woman cleared her throat. "Mm, no I don't think so," she said. The tone of her voice was solid. Her eyes were crystal blue and she looked -for Abbey usually decided these things at a glance- decent.

Bee turned away, toward the bartender. The woman in the suit was quick not to let her stray too far and engaged her further -a good sign. "Do I look familiar?"

Bee faced her again. "Nn, I thought so." She looked her over a little more. "But I guess not... Well. I'm Abbey. It's nice to finally meet you."

"Pam. Join me?"

Bee nodded and took a seat, the curve of her smile turning just so.

"Taking a break from politics?" Pam asked, gesturing toward the musicians.

True, there wasn't so much D.C. banter echoing wall to wall in this particular club, and it was nice that way. "Oh, I'm not in politics," Bee said.

She smirked, "That makes my line: 'Uh well I do beg your pardon, but *everybody's in politics...*'"

Laughing with her, Bee watched the earlier glint of light now spark in the hue of her eyes. Again, the rasp of the saxophone glided.

"I'm a lawyer," Pam said. "From south of Alexandria. I come in town once a week or so." She waited as Abbey sipped her wine. "And what is it that you do?"

Bee was glad for the leading question -it gave her something to work with. Letting the wine glass linger at her lips a moment longer, she gauged the blue eyes a little more then said, "Hmm... I do quite a number of things, Pam." And she paused. "I'm a senior editor of a women's magazine. I'm here verifying some stories."

"Oh yeah? What magazine?"

"I don't really want to talk about that." And she waited to see how Pam would respond. Sure enough, the woman from Alexandria was willing to play. 'Damn!' Abbey thought to herself once again, '*I am on a roll...*'

They talked awhile longer, Pam ordered more wine and leaned in closer behind Bee as they quieted to attend the jazz. The sultry play of notes continued, perfect with the work of the wine... Catching the fragrance of the woman beside her, Abbey found herself utterly relaxed. A few minutes later she turned and whispered close in her ear: "Let's get a cab?"

Just outside the club the lawyer took her first kiss. It was wonderful,

Abbey thought. Forceful and impassioned… sexy enough to let her know Pam wanted her, restrained enough to impart there were still details yet to unfold. In the cab Pam was rather gentle, lighter kisses and a soft touch to the shoulder strap of Bee's dress. Abbey pulled close and gave a squeeze at the Italian fabric at Pam's thigh. "Don't you dare be shy with me," she whispered. "I promise I won't either." And she savored the quick evolution of the lawyer's expression, spotlighted by the skipping pulse of the passing streetlamps.

The dream was about a simple box… the cigar box she'd gotten back at the estate sale. But in the dream there was a lock on it, and Bee had to pry it open, ravenously curious to see what lay hidden within.

For hours it seemed she was prying the thing. A kitchen knife, a pair of pliers, then dream-time implements: a crayon, a magic wand, a flower, a feather… It was at last the feather that turned it. And then the dream exploded.

A flashing series of motions and feelings came down, one after the other and again. With the turn of the feather, Abbey opened her box and at once there was a scream somewhere and a flood of water that knocked her feet out from under her. People kept screaming and calling -no one was hurt but there was a high urgency- and Abbey pulled herself upright to go to them. The water kept coming, and important things were washing away: the cigar box, the baby blanket she'd passed down to Molly, piano keys, forks and spoons and then bricks and cement from the house…

The calls kept coming: her mother, her boss, distant friends, past lovers, grandparents and cousins... Molly and Greta were not there; they were somewhere safe Abbey knew. Her mother's cry came again. And again.

'Shut up,' Abbey called back. 'Shut up, shut up, I can't hear Dad! Where is he? -Dad? D- *Shut up!!"*

And she woke herself, muttering aloud and sweating, teeth clenched. It was still dark outside the hotel window and Pam was beside her; she ran a hand over the woman's shoulder to secure herself and drew in deep breaths. The fragrance of Pam's hair and skin, so close now, brought their night's lovemaking instead into her thoughts and it calmed Abbey.

But where was her father? He'd been so far away in the dream, so out of reach. It brought on an old sadness. And more thoughts too: Her mother, her cousin Mackie... Ben Cole had been there for Christ's sake... and Brian, Molly's dad... *But where was her own father?*

Abbey breathed deep again and for a few minutes she simply lay there. Then she rolled to her side, wrapping herself close next to Pam. She and Brian had started this way too, strangers then bed-buddies and then somehow parents-to-be. There had been details in between of course, though not many. -Hints of love, notions of commitment... Brian had even proposed.

"Ahhhhh-" Pam was stirring, half-awake. Abbey thought to herself how it had been years since Brian... And she nudged herself forward and pressed her tongue to Pam's mouth.

"And so the next day..?" Greta was asking. "Things didn't go so easy, did they?"

And Abbey recounted details. The confrontation with the writer -which drew out into a second confrontation the following morning...
Waiting in offices for brief face-to-face moments... Phone calls. A grinding conversation with the Vice President, Edward Endeen... Two days' delay and one elusive loose end.

"So you had to can one of the stories? That's not so bad is it?"

"Ultimately, no. Catching a possible series of misquotes before going to print is a good thing, of course. Bad circumstances, though. And it's never fun to fire somebody, even if she was just a freelancer."

"And now the boss knows the truth about you-"

Abbey raised a brow.

"-that you're not able to work miracles, not all the time." Greta smiled with that knowing crook to her expression.

Bee grimaced at her.

"And did you go out and meet somebody here or there?"

"Oh I went out, sure. The bustle of D.C., you know... it's exciting. Reminds me of Manhattan, so I had a good time."

Greta's stare held.

"But no one special," Abbey obliged. Her tone was light, but final.

Instinctively Greta knew there was more, but let the conversation to its own. There was a pause, then Abbey thanked her again for taking care of Molly, and she pulled a little gift box from her tote bag. "Really, Greta," the woman reiterated, "I appreciate all the love you give Molly. And how safe I know she is with you. Thank you."

Chapter Six

The month's issue of *Mosaic* went to print, and everything calmed down at work. Little Molly wanted to be a gypsy for Halloween: she and Greta colored and painted and made the costume by day, at night Bee helped finish up some of the details. They visited Bonaday's for an annual party and drew faces on pumpkins, played games and ate a special orange-themed feast.

Beginning in November the sky seemed to hang lower and the world outside slowed… There was more darkness and a quiet peace too, day after day toward winter. Abbey Taft had never been one to particularly like or dislike this time of year, but the calm of this November was somehow sweet and soothing to her. -Except for the dreams that kept coming.

Every few nights she'd awaken, jarred, ignited with strange fever. Most of the dreams she could not remember. That, she thought, made them worse. Then suddenly the dreams stopped, and that seemed bad too. Abbey's puzzlement about them continued though she dared not ask Greta for any insights… It was a mix of things, the fever and the dreams; a mix that made her anxious yet amused. Something of it all made her giggle once or twice, there in the darkness past midnight, wondering. And the mystery somehow added to the season.

"Mom, sit here."

"T.V."

"No, Mom, the t.v.'s going off. It's time to eat now. Thanksgiving dinner, remember? Molly, tell your grandma what's for dinner on Thanksgiving."

"Turkey, Gramma! And canned berry sauce and sweet potatoes with marshmallows. -Bread," she continued, "and butter... Beans and stuffing and..."

Abbey rounded the couch to grasp her mother's shoulders and guide her toward the kitchen. "Dinner, Mommy," she whispered to the old woman. "C'mon."

"-olives and salt and pepper and gravy! Ooh and pie, Gramma, lots of pie!"

The dinner gathering was small this year, just the three of them, though Bee thought it was special. Earlier she'd propped up the tripod and taken a few pictures of them all, dressed up and together this way. At the table they had sparkling grape juice, but Abbey fully planned to nip at the gin a little later. For now she raised a toast, seated here between the generations:

"To my Mom and to my Molly, I am thankful for-"

"Turkey!" the little girl squealed.

At once Caroline chimed in, "Turkey, cranberry sauce, sweet potatoes with marshmallows…" reciting verbatim the order Molly had given. "…Bread and butter, beans and stuffing!" Her voice rose louder and louder. Molly giggled and joined in, "-And pie, lots of pie!!"

Despite the noise, Bee managed a smile and, after the pause, raised her glass once more. "Yes but *I* am thankful for-"

"Turkey," Caroline began. "Cranberry sauce, sweet potatoes with marshmallows, bread and butter, beans and stuffing, olives and salt and pepper, gravy and pie, lots of pie!"

Molly was hysterical, but Bee quieted her with a solid glance. Over and over, Caroline went through the menu. Abbey waited out her mother and once the silence came again stared at her directly. "Holy crap, Mom, you can remember that but you can't even remember we eat Thanksgiving dinner at the dining room table and not in front of the television? How important a day you made sure it was in the family you demanded that we pretend to be every holiday? Or how important the piano was? And the precious songbooks and sheet music? -How many damn hours you spent telling me how musically inferior I am? Recite that for me, Mom: *Every Good Boy Does Fine…* Can't remember?!" Abbey caught a glimpse of Molly, frightened and shrinking in her chair. "-Shit," the woman finished. And she began serving the dinner.

That night there were no bad dreams but Abbey spent a long time thinking about her mother and father and the relationship they had created for themselves, as well as the one they had presented all those years. They had never been the type to be particularly façadic, but there was always a different view as the adult looking back than as the child living through. And tonight Abbey took time to consider it.

Her father had been the son of a farmer, generally a kind man though sometimes aloof and distant. Abbey wondered now if it was bouts of depression that had plagued and haunted him. Her mother was intelligent -partial to cynicism- and a woman trapped in time. She'd gotten her master's degree and taught mathematics for a year and a half, then had been expected to become a housewife after the marriage.

In their early years together, the young Tafts had bordered on penniless. Abbey imagined that was the place where her mother's judgmentalism had been seeded. -Not out of the unique pain that poverty can bring… but from the worry and awkward fear that others might find out about it.

And so Caroline Taft prodded her children forward through the years with deliberateness and a close watchful eye. It became at times a strangle-hold. She was like a trainer, obsessed with final victory. The softer side of mothering showed through on occasion, but not often. Abbey imagined, looking back, that the tenderness rarely went out to her father either.

And Donald Taft receded. He grew tired under the weight of struggling for money; struggling to keep his good humor intact; struggling against the expectations his wife held for the family. He lost his boundaries. Abbey remembered that clearly. She'd thought he was a weak man and she'd resented him most of her life. His distance, his charged flares that came sometimes… Later he mellowed and his humor came back, but it was a short few years before he died and was gone.

Bee rarely thought about the old dynamics; it brought a unique pain. Tonight however she tried to keep a bit of perspective. It soothed her awhile, until she thought about her mother now: symptoms of the Alzheimer's, symptoms of the years gone by... She wondered if she would be impatient with her father, if he were here now instead. Would she be quite so angry with him for forgetting the past details that had been so damned important once upon a time?... Would she find herself judging him for allowing the excuse of old age to free him forever from having to say things that had never been said? -or was the judgmentalism a bond reserved just for mother and daughter? ...Abbey wondered.

And words she'd heard recently floated by... on a current that seemed soft and tempting yet alive with the kind of truth-rhythm that makes one tremble.

:*'You'll want to break through some of this fog, Abbey, so that it doesn't descend unto your daughter as well. These things truly can be passed down. Usually they are, as a matter of course.'* And there was more, the final beat: *'You won't want that to happen again.'*

She tried to remember if a ghost had said that to her, or more likely one of the dreams. -It was a haunting 42 words.

-Cancer, Abbey thought a little glibly, now that's something not to pass down. Bad teeth, maybe. A poor musical ear... *but this??* I don't even know what it is, she thought. Fog and feelings and uncertainty...

Suddenly the vision flashed: Molly in her chair at the table tonight, at first alight with laughter and four-year-old glee watching her grandma and silliness alive across the table... abruptly muted and turned to a shrinking, frightened squint as she sighted her mother and pain.

"Whether I like it or not," Bee said aloud to herself, "I am here right between them. On course to become her, on course to become *me*..."

Her throat went a little dry and her chest felt heavy. -What, in fact, was so bad about a little girl seeing her grandma being silly? God knew, Abbey herself never saw such a thing.

...Sleep came eventually, restful as it was lying tight, straight and stiff. And the dreams too were gone.

Deadlines for the next issue of the magazine fell around Christmas Day. The issue was not nearly as complex but many of the *Mosaic* staff were off on holiday breaks. Abbey found herself staying late hours and volunteering for an extra project or two. It showed in her holiday bonus, and these were the marks she chose to keep in mind... very clear and focused, well away from any foggier details.

She thought about how to spend the bonus money, possibly taking a family cruise early next year and whether or not to invite Greta... She bought Molly her first computer for Christmas and spent night after night playing learning-games with the little girl. A great production of Jekyll and Hyde was in town -Abbey found herself a blind date and went. There was a conference in Manhattan. And around the first of February some of the little things one of her junior editors continued to waste time on defeated Abbey's patience. Bee fired him, enduring the extra workload... and ignored the wise glances from Greta who kept finding ways to make mention of the finer tricks of timing;

coincidence; subconscious avoidance; spinning tires. Abbey rebutted that 'life is life sometimes' and sure enough in mid-March took Molly on the cruise. Just the two of them.

"Mol-ly-" Abbey called, a pleasant singsong to her tone. The little girl bounced down the stairs and asked what her mother wanted.

"Remember, it's Saturday? We're going to start working the garden today, just like last year. Let's go, put on your boots!"

Excitedly the child did so, and took Bee's outstretched hand as they headed to the yard. In their windbreakers and matching baseball caps they grabbed shovels and hoe and took to the soil. Before too long Molly was busy not with tilling, but with the science of measuring worms. Abbey laughed and noticed the sheen of sunlight on the melting ice-water in the birdbath. There was a glistening light about her daughter, a glistening light to the day…

'It would be sad for the fog to come down here and now,' she might have thought.

But today, for today, such a thing did not cross her mind.

"C - Do you remember how to make a 'c'?" she was asking, calling to Molly from across the kitchen, later that afternoon.

"Yes Mommy, I can do it!" The four-and-a-half year old proudly held up the ice cream stick, a unique little scribble there on its end.

"And 'c' is for c-c-c… *carrots*," Abbey told her.

"Kay I'll get an orange crayon."

"And what's on the top of a carrot? What color grows on top of the ground, do you remember? You pull a carrot up by its top and the top is…"

"Green!"

"Good, Molly! Good remembering."

Carefully the child colored two spots on the end of her stick, alongside the scribble: orange and green.

"Well you have been a really good helper today, Kiddo," Bee said, rounding the table and handing off two quarters. "Thank you."

Molly's eyes widened. "Ooh, Mommy…" And with a little twitch of wonder she glanced to the curio cabinet nearby. "But can I trade for pennies?"

Obliging, Abbey retrieved the antique toy bank from the cabinet, setting it and two smaller sized coins before the child. Tiny clown hands clapped, demanding the deposit. Molly pressed down her copper and the clown flipped it with a soft mechanical whoosh. Losing a breath, little Molly did it again, then looked up to her mommy and giggled.

Abbey smiled, watching close as Molly studied the bank, a little scared to touch too hard but very curious about the whole works: how the coins flipped, where they were hidden, if the clown was real… Bee studied along with her, recalling the estate sale and where this bank came from. She left the toy on the table a few days. Then one day, midst cleaning, it was set back into the cabinet once again.

Chapter Seven

It was a greater chore, but Bee decided this time to visit Bonaday's alone. Her mother was in a quiet mood, and it was well after supper so there was a coziness to the evening. There in Caroline's mini-apartment, they propped up on the bed together and looked at t.v.

A game show droned, but it soothed Abbey. And her mother giggled a little at the contestants and the flash of colors on the screen. Her chuckle and intent hold at the glow of the television was something like Molly's. Occasionally the silver-haired woman blurted an answer to one of the questions. More than not, she was right.

Abbey simply sat, watched, closed her eyes a bit, listened… And she let the words, "I miss you sometimes, Mom," fall from her mouth. When she added, "And I miss Daddy," Caroline turned to her, expression soft, and reached for her daughter's hand.

The moment wasn't long, but it was something. Not a minute passed and Caroline was commenting on the red of Abbey's nail color.

"You don't approve?" Bee smiled. "It seems a bit strong, huh Mom…" And she squeezed her hand in return. "There are so many things I wish we could talk about. -My work... What this nail color is supposed to represent there. How all that crap is hard... I know part of you envies me my independence and my career; I wish you could live some of this through me, maybe it'd be thrilling for you and a nice companionship for me."

Abbey sighed. The t.v. had the greater part of her mother's attention- the game show host to be exact. But they were still holding hands, and they were here together. And that had to be something.

Making her way back home that night, Abbey realized just how warm the spring air had finally turned. The teapot beckoned; she toted a wrap and her mug out to the back porch. There were night sounds, and the quiet dark sky was dotted with stars. The moths had returned for the season and off in the neighbor's yard a first frog chirped. Bee considered just how friendly the silences had become this winter... she wondered if the new spring would bring a change.

Then another thought crossed her mind: the busy-ness at work, and beyond work, and how that motion was a different kind of silence. It was easy, she knew, to overlook the difference.

A soft breeze billowed, making the chimes ring out by the garden. Abbey breathed in the nighttime -all the scents, every one... deeply, deeply.

Molly wakened when the piano sounded; it made her smile. Her mother was playing the Moonlight Sonata. The notes were soothing, and the notes were strong.

"Yes Mommy, let's measure worms!" Molly darted outside, along with her playmate Alison. The girls scooted to the shed, pulled on colorful gloves and ran out to the patch of the garden. Abbey followed and, handful after handful, mulch was added to the beds. Proudly, Molly showed her friend how to re-set the little wooden sticks and explained the rows of seeds that had been planted underneath. The two sang rhymes from this week's preschool class, then Bee asked for more details.

"...Well, Camden found a nest for bees and we got to touch it. And Sadie got back from chicken pox. Mommy? ...why do chickens do that to kids?"

Abbey laughed, but said outright she just didn't know. Young Alison meekly added, "I'm a veggie-tarian... so I won't get chicken pox." Then she squealed at Molly, "Don't you hurt those worms, Molly Taft! Here, hold him like this..."

A soft breeze blew. It reminded Abbey of the night before, though the scents today were different. Sun-dried soil, the earthiness of dirty hands and the damp mulch... Green was beginning to emerge here and there about the yard; it too had a fragrance all its own. Something like-

The breeze blew again, and the chimes danced then chinked in their thick-toned melody. There were several hung just near the garden, under the eaves of the shed, and today Bee edged toward them curiously. The worn keys on the fishing line, from the estate sale, made little noise together but they spun in the wind. They did not sparkle in the new sunlight like the other metal chimes; the keys were too rusted or tarnished. Even the bent trio of forks at the top had lost its shine.

Yet someone had taken care to fashion that fishing line all together, in anticipation of making simple music, and that of course had a shine all its own. Smiling, Abbey remembered the day at the estate sale, her visions of the old couple who had once lived there, and a thought or two about her birthday.

She fingered the handmade chime. And something caught her attention.

They were antique keys, most of them, with long slender posts or thick hand-forged curves and worn smooth spots here and there where thumbprints might be seen, mismatched, if time would allow such sights. A few had a little etching work or even a number printed on one side. But one, dangling there no more or less out of place than any of the others, was indeed different.

Abbey pulled the lot down altogether and went back to the porch. Sitting, she took a drink of her soda and fingered through the keys one by one. Sure enough, there midst all the others, was something not quite antique. Little numbers were stamped on one side: three of them. '2-3-3.' And the letters across the little key's face read 'PO Wltn Tnshp.'

Molly hopped up beside her mother. "Whatcha doin, Mommy? We're hungry."

"Mm..." Abbey was thinking.

"Mommy? My tummy is talking."

Bee finally faced her. "Okay, Kiddo. Let's get some peanut butter and jelly for you and Alison."

All through lunch the girls chattered, but Abbey only pretended to listen. The key had struck her, though she wasn't sure why.

Whelton Township… She'd driven through a few times and there wasn't much to it. Very quaint, she recalled, with a wide creek running alongside Main Street and a stoplight or two to mark the center of town.

2-3-3. Something about that struck her too, seemingly familiar. Maybe an old area code or some series on a license plate…

Molly broke her thoughts. "Can we, Mommy, can we?"

"What?"

"A movie, can we go watch one?"

"You can later. Now go get your jackets and use the potty. We're gonna go out and get some ice cream."

'So what was it that made you decide to drive out right then and there?' she could imagine Greta asking. Throughout the long ride, Bee herself wondered. It was a strange thing: the key itself, her curiosity about it… the months that had gone by.

It was Spring. The sky was clear and blue, no sign of rain, no sign of fog. There were two giggling girls with ice cream cones in the back seat. And Abbey had a key in her hand and a fascination; a new drive to the hours of this day. -It felt like the break of silence indeed.

Chapter Eight

That Saturday night Greta herself got a phone call. She hurried across town knowing little else beyond the tone of Abbey Taft's voice.

"And so you went out to the post office..."

"It was closed, you know, but there was open access to the mailboxes. I had this key, Greta, and I went in -I don't really know why- but I..." Bee stopped altogether, her stare held unwavering. Across the kitchen table Greta watched as a tear angled down the woman's face.

"The key fit..." Greta knew, prodding her.

Slowly, Abbey nodded. Her eyes were filled with such intensity: wonder, fear, disbelief... The extremes pulled at her, so unfamiliar, and another tear drew slowly down.

"The key fit..." Greta said again.

"Yeah. I put the key in, and it turned, though it was a little stuck. Kind of rusted or something. But it turned pretty easy, I mean, otherwise I'd just have walked away." Greta offered a gentle smile. After a pause, Bee continued, "So it turned, and I just opened it. I think I laughed a little, because it just seemed funny and odd and... I don't know. Then I saw all of it -the box was crammed full, Greta. Crammed. I pulled at one envelope, because I was so curious about whose box it could be after all that, you know, but just one letter wouldn't come free. It was too full. So a bunch tumbled out. And I remember catching a glimpse as one creamy envelope fell out and down to the floor... I could read it as it fell away from me, like slow motion... *It was addressed to me.*"

Greta gasped outright. "Have you ever been there, to Whelton?"

"I've never registered for a PO Box, if that's what you mean. Here-"

With that she slipped something across the table. It was the cream colored envelope. The little 13¢ stamp first caught Greta's attention. Out of place, yet familiar in a nostalgic sort of way. And the address in the middle of the envelope read, in block letters:

> Post Office Box 233
> Abbey Taft

Again she gasped. "Who is it from?"

With a gesture Abbey motioned for her to take a look. Gingerly, Greta pulled the single page letter free. The paper was brittle and the creases were well-set. It was blank stationery, with lines, and the edges were turning brown. The block letters were child-like:

> Dear Abbey,
> I am writing this becaus you hurt my feelings today.
> Why do you do that? You are not any better than me.

I think your dumb. I think your scared even, that's why

you do say things like that. Well I'm not scared.

And I'm not your freind anymore either.

Dawn Ballard

"Well, who is Dawn Ballard?"

"She's somebody I knew in 2nd grade I think. Or 3rd grade." Bee
reached for her mug of coffee and sipped long.

"So she sent this to you because…?"

"She never sent this to me, Greta, I've never seen it before." Her tone
rose, and she pulled a full handful of envelopes from her satchel.

"Look at these! -My cousin, another one from Dawn Ballard, some boy
I don't remember, my mom, a teacher, a babysitter… It's fucking crazy,
Greta!" And her eyes flared; the tears had changed form.

"It's kind of neat, really," Greta said, trying again to smile.

But Abbey was not swayed. "It's freaky!!"

Greta held. "What do the other ones say?" And she swept some of
them closer with a motion across the table.

"Wait a minute." And Abbey stared at her friend, eyeing the woman's
set expression. Then she asked, "What was that psychic's name?"

"You mean Catherine?"

"I need her number."

Greta nodded, then squinted up at the new flash in Bee's eye. "Why are
you looking like that, Abbey? That's a new look for you…" Again,
she tried some levity and calm, but Bee did not respond. "Do you think

Catherine had something to do with this?"

Bee blinked, but was quick to reply, "Get her number please."

Greta didn't move toward her purse; instead she studied Bee a little longer. "You think I had something to do with this, don't you?" And her tone was sharp.

"Obviously someone did."

The hurt and disbelief Greta initially felt slipped quickly away, and she found herself laughing. Quietly, respectful for Abbey's confusion, but laughing just the same. And she retrieved her purse, then walked to Abbey and took her hand as she passed over the psychic's phone number. "Call her," Greta said, squeezing Bee's palm, "but she'll tell you what I'm about to: I had nothing at all to do with this. I couldn't have thought it up -it's so… involved… And you know me, Bee, I would never trespass on your feelings like this. I might dole out advice, I might get cocky sometimes but it's always to your face, you know that. I would never presume to rummage through your past. That's really only something each of us can do for ourselves."

Abbey blinked again, and softened somewhat. She exhaled a long breath then shrank back into her chair. Greta reached for her shoulder and squeezed, a massaging and soothing motion. "Why don't we put the 'how' of this aside for a second? Have you read all of the letters?"

The woman nodded, her gaze misted again. She would not face Greta.

"They made you sad?"

Abbey paused, and a flurry of adverbs blew in, like snowflakes. Windblown, weary, unsure, exhausted, weak, agitated, sorry, torn, frantic, bewildered… And the words fell atop one another, growing, banking… *growing*. Abbey cut them short and answered out loud, "They made me… tired."

After a long silence, she chose another letter and read it to Greta. Then another. After a third, she paused again, and added kahlua to her coffee. "It's funny, isn't it," she acknowledged, "how I feel tired and confused and weak, even mad… but how I might instead feel excitement or anticipation or something, you know?"

Greta's brown eyes kindly glistened.

"Treasures…" Abbey said, fingering the pages. "Treasures, all." The tone of her sarcasm was sharp, but shaky. And the point of her outstretched fingers fell limp. She exhaled a long sigh, facing her friend.

There was a pause.

"I'm not very good at being vulnerable, although that's not a surprise I thought I'd go ahead and admit it…. Thanks, Greta, for not looking at me like you're looking through me. I-"

"Hey," Greta said softly. "You have a past. Just like the rest of us. And these might make you feel vulnerable but they're not bad. They're fine, you know? They're just… letters." She cocked her head. "They're *amazing*, but they're just letters."

Then she asked if Abbey was okay, and stood to go. "We'll talk some more about it. Soon." And she smiled, and left Bee to finish the last draught of coffee.

It was strange for Bee that she found it hard on Monday to simply go back to work.

That she dwelt on other thoughts, on other feelings than those that awaited at her desk was an altogether new venture. She had many obligations, but tried to focus on the busy work -it made her simper at one point to think that today like, perhaps, so many of the employees she'd worked with throughout the years, she herself wished only to ride the clock. Keep busy, pass the minutes and hours, remain thoughtless when possible, collect the coins at the end of the day.

"Well the damn letters have achieved something," she whispered over a report just before four o'clock. "Here I am, possibly in fellowship with more of my co-workers than ever before..."

And words from the mysterious pages shot across her mind: *'Why do you do that? You are not any better than me...'* Abbey rose abruptly and marched herself to the water cooler down the hall. A break, a different focal point, a moment's clear goal, a purposeful momentum. "It is fine," she told herself, remembering instead a word or two from Greta Duvall, and squinted closed her eyes a moment. "Everything is just fine."

After several days of uneasiness and near overwhelm, Abbey decided she had to strategize, put something in place so she could feel better about all this; settle into some semblance of understanding it all.

Night after night she came directly home from work, checked in briefly with Greta, played with Molly and sipped at wine or coffee while staring long hours at the fireplace in the living room. She turned on the t.v. occasionally, that was all. That, and the thoughts she let come and go. "Forming a strategy," she would tell herself. "Getting a damn handle on things..."

New information. *Old* information It had jostled her equilibrium. And Abbey Taft wasn't used to feeling so. Ultimately the decision came to pick one letter at a time, randomly, and figure out why it affected her. She would give it several days, take it apart word by word if necessary, until the thing felt less weighted; less charged.

The one that seemed the oldest was handwritten by her mother. Coincidentally, it was the first one chosen.

> Dear Little Abbey,
>
> You are our special girl, right in the middle.
> Three years younger than Katie, five older than
> your new brother Caleb. You have a perfect place
> right in between, you get to be a little sister and
> a big sister all at the same time!
>> We love you,
>> Mom and Dad

Nothing about this one confused Abbey nor felt heavy. The words simply made her cry.

She sat in the recliner with a box of tissues, and when the tears didn't stop she retrieved an old photo album as well. There she sat, in faded hues of an old polaroid print, the new baby Cale wrapped in her arms. She was five, and her feet dangled over the edge of the couch. Katie sat alongside, a goofy smile as she vied for attention. Daddy and Mom were in the next picture by themselves with their little bundled newborn.

Thirty-seven years ago... Now the baby in the photo was a young investment banker, Kate with the goofy smile was still vying for attention and raising two boys of her own, and Abbey was wondering, tearful on a late Thursday night, just what in fact her place really was all along after all...

It had never much bothered her to be in the middle; it had never much made a difference. Having a sister, having a brother... Parents who were reasonably happy though not ecstatically so... Parents who might have been happier had they not boarded themselves into the time and place of all their circumstances. It was never really a thing of question -just family, *her* family... But those thoughts didn't linger much tonight. Tonight simply came the tears.

Indeed, the next day at work did seem better. She saw a woman she vaguely knew -Janine- down at the snack shop, who was looking a little bleary-eyed today and somehow obsessed over finding just the right chewing gum. Nervously, Janine said hello and engaged in a quick moment's conversation with Abbey. Something about it brought Bee to thoughts of her sister. She wished she had the courage -and the necessary tact- to pull Janine aside just then and there and put to her outright, 'Tell me in three sentences what exactly was missing between you and your parents. *What was it that was missing??*'

And suddenly something like a ghost appeared for a minute, there near the counter at the snack shop. It was vague and diffuse and unrecognizable. '...How to define that which is missing...' Bee thought to herself. And the wisp of a phantom disappeared.

Her thought repeated however, and she carried it with her back up the elevator. Today it was the sort of thought that fueled her, well beyond the heaviness of days' past.

Another thought came and with it, a smile made its way across Bee's face... She felt as if there was a key in her hand, suddenly. And it was warm and pulsing, as if with life. 'Perhaps the key was the most important find of all. Not the mailbox, not even the letters...' And she wasn't quite sure if this was in fact a thought of her own, or the shadow of the ghost making mention...

Her smile widened, despite stares in her direction getting off the elevator. Indeed, these were the private little mysteries worth taking 10 minutes' break for, she told herself. And the decision was made to carry the Whelton Township key in her pocket or on a chain in the days yet to come.

Dear Abbey Taft,

You sing good.

I wanna be your frend.

Jeffrey

This letter could have been easy to dismiss. -Simple, common as six-year-old thought would go... it did not bring much puzzlement nor did it bring tears to Abbey. But she could not set it aside without consideration, for it too had had a place in the mailbox.

And so, night after night, Bee pondered the twelve words. She pushed grey memories into colored flashes, trying to come across an idea of what little Jeffrey had looked like. -Had he been in her kindergarten class? First grade? Maybe the Sunday school she'd visited a dozen times or so... Had there been something else? The recognition of dance lessons skittered through her memory... it was something she barely remembered, but had that been all? Perhaps there was dance as well as music: singing...

But she was not sure. Nor did she know why it quite mattered anyway. Yet it pulled at her. Jeffrey.

One morning in the shower she thanked him out loud, the little featureless boy who wanted to befriend her. "I'm sure you're sweet and important and I thank you for your kindness and this message," she said to him.

And that evening, playing with Molly and her dollhouse, Bee re-named the littlest baby boy doll. Molly just giggled. She liked the new name.

Chapter Nine

The shuffle of work soon caught Bee up again, carrying her like a tide. Late April deadlines were upon her, though the *Mosaic* issue was coming together this month with only very minor difficulties. When the phone rang this morning the woman brightened with a familiar surge of momentum and anticipation: this cascade, she remembered, was exactly why she loved her high-powered career. Endeen needed something. Bee saw to it immediately in a series of well-maneuvered phone calls. By 10am the thing was handled, and Abbey was invigorated. She asked her assistant to re-schedule her one o'clock appointment and book a long lunch meeting instead, reward for the renewal she was feeling.

Next to Greta, John Jaffers was Bee's most brilliant friend. Almost an accomplice really, the two of them had known each other since Minneapolis. They had kissed, but only once, and remained close friends these twenty years though on occasion there were stretches of months and months between contact.

"...The worst and best thing I think we ever did," John was saying, today over a meatball sandwich and fries, "was that time we had the double date with Stephanie and Nathan… and you begged me to let you spend the better part of the evening flirting with Stephanie. And there was poor Nathan, who had no inclinations whatsoever, trying to worry about whether or not I was going to reach for his thigh or something over dinner…" He laughed. "Poor guy, I'm sure he still has night sweats over that. I mean truly, Abbey Dear, you were absolutely awful to that young man."

Bee chuckled along, sipping at her soda. "He asked me out to get ahead at the office; it was obvious. You know I hate that kind of game-playing… You and I handled that night like clockwork. It was beautiful. The only low point to it was the fact that Stephanie wasn't in on it from the beginning…" And she chuckled again, remembering details. "My nanny never believes that story. She finds it hard to believe I have that kind of prankster in me."

"That's why you get away with things. You just don't look the part. That's why you're dangerous." And he winked at her, smug, taking a gulp of the sandwich.

"So how is Susan?" Abbey asked.

"Oh, she's well. Off to another seminar this week. But we're good. And you dating anybody, My Princess?"

"No…" And she sighed the word, though dating wasn't something she longed for. John was well aware of that, but he dug for a few related details anyway.

"Well you been getting laid then?"

She giggled. "I love you, John."

His expression brightened to hear it. "But answer the bloody question," he pressed, feigning a British accent.

And she acquiesced, telling him there'd been a couple of one-night rendezvous. He nodded proudly, then changed the subject.

His wife was a doctor, and John loved to divulge some of the research she was doing. The workings of the human capacity for illness and injury then for healing itself fascinated him. For quite some time now Susan Jaffers studied tissue regeneration, including steps beyond regeneration into cloning and seeding new tissue altogether. On the other end of the conversation, today as well as any day, Abbey happily engaged him. -To see the marvel in his eyes that was simply love for his wife, truly... it in turn fascinated Abbey. At one point during the conversation she wondered if John realized it, or whether he was under the impression that Bee continued all these years to find cloning and the research itself as interesting as he did. And she studied him, and wondered, but decided not to ask about it.

Instead she commented, "You know, it's great how proud you are of Susan. I'm happy for you. For both of you."

John grinned wide. There was a pause, then he asked about her own work.

"I've had some time feeling a little bit off," she said, never mentioning the letters, "but I'm back to myself again. This morning Endeen called with an article fallen through; I cleared it up in an hour and it was a rush. For three days he's had somebody else looking into it... then he tells me and I work it out like that -one call to the writer, two to the sources, one to Ben Cole... Bam, bam, bam."

After nodding acknowledgment, John put to her, "Ah, Ben Cole, the freelancer. The mysterious, wonderful, slightly effeminate but dark and dependable Benjamin Cole..."

Abbey raised a brow.

"Well, if he asked you out would you indeed say yes?"

"Do you know something I don't, Mr. Jaffers?"

He only shrugged his shoulders. "How about Endeen himself?"

Bee snapped a potato chip, unable to say the words fast enough. "God no, not Edward. He's married anyway." Then she chewed a bit more delicately, and thoughtfully gazed past John for a moment toward the window. "But no," she finally said, "I don't think I'd go out with Ben either. Because I know he'd be serious -I mean seriously interested in me- and really, John, I'm not wanting to settle down right now."

She chose her words carefully. It wasn't the settling down that discouraged her... there was something else to it. But John was satisfied. He asked a couple more questions, and that was all.

Abbey returned to the office in a different mood altogether. She was energized certainly -spending time with John was always a good thing- but this new secrecy she was putting to him... it couldn't last, of course. John knew her too well. But in the meantime she felt like a liar. That she had been drawn to behave so had her perplexed, a sensation little different than those that had accompanied the letters in the first place.

That night, there were dreams again. One struck her most of all: she was in a shower at her old apartment in Manhattan, and she kept trying to wash, to lather herself and spray the water hard and fast. Over and over again, she kept getting in and out of the stall, but never did she feel completely clean.

Waking, she found herself sweaty. Sticky and uncomfortable. "This is what lying feels like," she told herself. But another voice edged in, somewhere through the fog of her thoughts as she woke fully: 'This is what the truth feels like, this is how the truth feels...'

Her own shower that morning was short. Desperately hot, then to icy cold. The shock sent a pain up and down her back and over her scalp; something basic and different to focus on. In the mirror Abbey's eyes looked back with a hue of darkened grey and she pushed herself to stare hard into the reflection. "Shit," she finally said. "Shit, I'm back here again already..."

Not long and Greta Duvall realized there was a conversation missing between her and Abbey. At least one, maybe more. But she decided to wait just a bit longer before bringing it up, to see if Bee herself might reach forward.

It was so unusual for Abbey Taft to call out sick from work that she did not even feel guilty about it, dialing from the cell phone as she drove along the highway. Besides, it simply seemed impossible for her to consider sitting behind that desk again with this flurry of emotions all about. The strange rises and ebbs, the unfamiliar hollow in her stomach... The sensations would have made it hard physically to sit still in her mahogany and leather chair all day. Ending the call, Abbey merged over into the turn lane and exited to head north.

It was a crisp but sunny day, and the park-like meadow beside Bonaday's was beautiful. Light dappled the newly green blades of grass and the yellow daffodils here and there. A few purple crocus remained midst the shade trees, adding pops of color, and a cement pathway curved in and around the grounds. Abbey pushed her mother Caroline in a wheelchair slowly through the morning. The sun made its course higher in the sky and there were long moments of silence between the two women.

"How was dinner last night?" Bee finally asked. "I saw on the schedule it was banana pudding night -your favorite. Was it good?"

Caroline didn't answer.

"Mom, you don't want to tell me about the banana pudding? I'd like to know if it was good."

Again, there was silence. A bird nearby fluttered and called; from the wheelchair Caroline gazed after the little creature and eventually pointed.

"A cardinal, hey Mom? Pretty red…"

The older woman turned in the chair, stretching to catch further sight. Abbey took time to realize how present the disease made her mother. There seemed little time except now in her quiet world. It was ironic, Bee thought, and she was brought to a memory:

At fifteen or sixteen it was all young Abbey could do to get her mother's attention on the day at hand unless, it seemed, to hold relevance toward some future outcome. 'Good grades today, good college tomorrow… Extra chores now to make extra time for the swim meet on Saturday…'

Another memory came like a blur suddenly: losing a high school boyfriend and feeling miserable. Her mom's only advice was to look ahead: 'In a few weeks you'll be at a dance and meet someone new…' There had been bitterness at her insensitivity; rebellion against her vision, so emotionless and pointed. And Abbey's father, ever busy with the day-to-day, never feeling able to look up or forward… How the young Abbey had wanted to side with him; how the extremes had hit hard at her teenage emotions.

In the end, she thought now, the two together created a hard-working and driven young daughter, sights in all directions. -Except toward the past, Bee now snickered, at least until just recently. How strange things were.

But now, here in the morning sunshine, Caroline Taft seemed only to focus on the cardinal flying by and the gentle spring air on her face. "Cold," she was saying, clapping her hands to warm them.

Abbey pushed her well out into the sun, locked the chair and sat across from the woman on a little park bench. Another bird swifted past, song on the wind. Together the two watched as it made its way toward the trees.

After awhile Abbey stared at her mother, watching the skin of her face that was now so much less familiar, with its soft wrinkles and greyish tone. She kept her mouth partially open much of the time and it appeared a little like a permanent look of surprise; very unfamiliar indeed. But it offered new insights.

"Mom," Bee said, "I want to talk to you, what do you think?"

Caroline met her stare and muttered agreement.

"Mom, I want to ask you about my dance class, about singing lessons, about what you thought it was like for me to be the middle child…" Her voice was calm and even, held from any urgency in that she didn't expect an answer.

Caroline looked away to smile at the birdsong again. Abbey gazed at her, wishing somehow that life and questions and explanations could in fact be as simple as that motion. –Into a brief smile and focused on flight and morning song…

There was a long moment then Caroline abruptly said, "Time to move, Abbey Elana. You are a good singer yes, but it's time to move." And she bent to release the brake of the wheelchair, urging her daughter on.

––––––––––––––––

Greta ordered Chinese food and invited herself for dinner. Molly chattered about the little boy named Camden who was in her class: "He has white-yellow hair, Mommy," she was saying. "Kind of like popcorn. Why don't kids have purple hair? or pink?"

After a short silence Abbey asked the child if she remembered what color cardinals were.

"Orange!" came the exclamation.

Bee smiled. "Very close… do you have another guess?"

"Red!"

"Bingo!" And she mentioned visiting Grandma today, having seen the little bird.

Greta cleared the dishes, re-appearing with a new coloring book she'd stashed in one of the cabinets. "Upstairs with your crayons, Molli-pop... I'll come say goodbye before I leave for home later.

"And you," she said with a turn back to Abbey, "I'm so glad you visited Caroline today, but-"

"But?"

"Isn't there something more to it?"

"Uh-mmm... Well, nothing more than the obvious."

"How are you doing, Bee, with the letters?"

Abbey shrugged. "Let's move into the living room."

Following, Greta reached a hand and patted her friend's back. "I'm proud of you," she offered. It sounded maternal, and struck a chord in Abbey that melted down walls.

"Well I've thought about some things, obviously... I've cried, I've sort of gotten a handle on them, I've been confused. I've been humbled, I've been overwhelmed... But you know the funniest thing, Greta, as logical as I am it's stopped crossing my mind at all to wonder why and how this whole thing happened."

Greta's smile went wide. "Then I am really proud of you." Her eyes glistened, a sincerity even deeper than that she interminably conveyed. After a pause, she asked how the day's visit had gone.

"Oh, Mom was good. I went in order to ask her something that had been in one of the letters. She answered, I guess, sort-of... Makes me wonder whose memory is- *Well*," and Bee smirked. "Anyway, the real lesson of the day turned out to be that I wasn't overly expectant so I could really see through and understand how different it is now. My mom, living utterly here and now, and that's all. It's so different. Usually I can't get past being resentful about it. You know, why the hell couldn't some of this have eeked into her life about thirty years ago? But, today was... new."

"Mm, I'm glad, Bee."

"Me too."

After another pause Greta said, "Have you been writing reply letters?"

Abbey cocked her head; clearly it hadn't occurred to her. She exchanged a thoughtful gaze with Greta, then Molly bounded down the stairs to show off her pictures.

On the elevator at work, Abbey happened to meet the woman again from the snack shop. It struck her, and she turned to ask Janine out sometime for a lunch date. Janine's eyes were a vast, scintillating green and she looked a little shaky again, just as she had that day last week. Abbey was honestly surprised when the young woman agreed to lunch.

"Maybe Thursday?" she asked.

Bee nodded.

"Great. I'll see you at 12:30? At the snack shop, we'll meet up front near the chewing gum. Think you can find it?" And her expression brightened with playfulness. Janine knew herself revealed, thought Bee. The openness there was amazing. It made Abbey curious to learn more. "We'll figure out where to go from there," she added, then headed back to work.

Thursday arrived. Bee found herself anticipating lunch with Janine, unlike other first meetings. Spending time with new acquaintances had rarely been Abbey Taft's forte -she lacked patience sometimes with the details of getting to know someone. But today things felt more interesting.

The morning moved quickly. There were conferences and work that was alive with urgency and import. Again, it invigorated Abbey. She met Janine with a liveliness of her own that afternoon and they wandered out to the deli.

"So, you're an editor with the magazine, right?"

"Yes. I've been with them about 3 ½ years now. Moved down from Manhattan when my daughter was born. I like *Mosaic*," and she slowed to say it again, "I like my work here."

Janine smiled. She was about thirty, and the age difference was something Abbey noted: it seemed intrinsic to that striking openness and the particular hue of her eyes. "Are you with the investment firm?"

"Yes. It's really kind of boring, but I've always liked math and probability and that kind of thing."

"My brother's an investment banker. And he always reassures me that handling people's money isn't necessarily boring."

"Well, I do forecasting. But yeah, ultimately it's money and that's exciting." She giggled in the wind and Abbey grinned with her.

A man held the door for them at the restaurant and they ordered at the counter. As they picked out a table Abbey thought of a few conversation starters -the thought returned to her about asking Janine direct and firm what had been missing between her and her parents; then suddenly she was snickering to herself and decided at once simply to stay quiet.

Janine instead mentioned her favorite dishes on the menu and sprinkled pepper onto her soup. There was a pause as they began eating, then she asked Bee about her daughter.

"Molly is her name. She'll be five in a few months. -I can't believe it. *Five...* Do you have kids?"

She pursed her lips. It was a look of sweetness, but something else too. "Yes, I have a baby boy. Garrett... he's fourteen months."

"I really like that age."

"Yeah, I wish he didn't have to be in daycare, away from me, but-" And she sighed, then spooned at the soup.

"Molly's done great with that. Almost all her life, five days a week, she's been at daycare or toddler camp or with her nanny. She's fine, Garrett will be fine too."

Facing her, the sweetness of Janine's expression was now clearly mixed with a pained intensity.

Bee was drawn to ask, "What is it?"

"I'm getting divorced," the young woman said, without much hesitation. "That's what I'm upset about. Joint custody, full-time daycare... I just miss him, you know?" And the green washed teary.

Abbey watched her a moment, then told her, "Hey, thanks for coming out today with all this going on."

"Oh." And Janine pressed her mouth into a smile. "Well, life goes on. And that's a good thing, it keeps me sane. And we don't have to talk about this. It just comes up, you know?"

Abbey agreed. There was a pause. "I'm trying to think of something funny to say from work. -Seems there's not much that's been very funny lately."

Across the table, Janine nodded at the attempt.

"Well, there is this thing that Molly has started." And Janine's grin widened to hear it. "She really wants a pet lately. So she does these things like draws ten little pictures so that when I come home I find a dog or a kitty on the stairs or in my bathroom… Molly says, 'See Mom, that's where Aspen would be right now.' In the family room, on his favorite chair…"

"Ahh, that's adorable Abbey. She's very clever."

"Yeah, that's not all. Ten minutes later she'll play a guessing-game with me about where we'll find Aspen next, then she runs around the house until she finds another one of her pictures… And she makes other things out of clay or a shoe box or something, like his little bed or even a litter box. She'll tell me at dinner, 'Oh Mommy, can I be excused? I have to go clean up Aspen's potty…' She's a little psychological wiz or something. She knows how she's getting her point across."

Janine laughed. "Kids are great. Even at Garrett's age, you see their little personalities and how adaptable and insightful they are. Molly sounds wonderful, she really does. Thanks, Abbey."

And they finished up their lunch with no more talk of divorce or family. Abbey thought about it later though, and throughout the day... *relationships, mirrors...* How complicated things seemed to get. Like a woven tapestry, many colors strong... many strands. Intertwined, connected, *individual strands ever separated...*

There was simplicity in the big picture, she knew. Days on holiday at the beach, observing the even rise and fall of the waves had taught that long ago. Cycles of the seasons, above and beyond details of this egg hatching and that one not... this tree growing and that one chopped... The big picture was whole and flat and no more or less beautiful.

It didn't take the wisdom of Greta Duvall to realize there were many perspectives, indeed: the tapestry under the microscope, the tapestry from afar.

Still, Janine's gaze came to mind, its inherent nature of wide open sincerity offering finer insight: a mix of sweetness and pain; a mix of clear sweetness and pain. Even from far across the restaurant today, Abbey would have noticed that incongruity.

The realization didn't bother her, but it stuck. Like a bite of tough steak, she kept chewing at it. And a long while later she'd abruptly remember it was there -something to ponder- to glean a little more nourishment from... somehow leaving an odd taste in her mouth.

That night Abbey found herself in the recliner after tucking Molly into bed. They'd played hide-and-seek for Aspen just after dinner and had put puzzles together before reading a bedtime story. Taking a moment now, Bee slowly exhaled. Then she pulled air in deep, deep into her lungs, finding it difficult to expand her abdomen fully. After a few more tries, the effort felt more complete and she closed her eyes, taking time to feel the light current of air through her nose and the pulse of the rhythm of her natural breaths.

After awhile, in a slow motion, she reached for the table and pulled a letter there free.

> Crabbey Abbey,
>
> You are such a brat! You always want
> things your way. Cale is the baby, not you
> so grow up.
>
> > Katie
> > P.S.- Leave my side
> > of the room alone!

Bee recalled how it must have been just about the same time this letter was written that her big sister went from being 'Katie' to 'Kate.' The older child had always known what she wanted, been outspoken and dominant. Later, as Caleb grew into a toddler, Katie seemed to realize more and more she was losing her hold in the spotlight... She'd gotten sillier, then serious to the extreme. By her mid-teens Kate -and only Kate- Taft was cut and dry and mundane. She gave up the sharpness instead for mediocrity, somehow finding that acting average got an attention all its own. Abbey had wondered about it, then and now. But tonight she also wondered what the effects were -not so much the behaving average, but the *expecting* average. How that had shifted Kate; how that had emptied her somehow and filled her with a new outlook for the world. Behind her eyes, it could always be noticed. That had become one reason Abbey grew distant from her sister: to be near Kate was to miss out on something; to realize something vital had gone.

In a motion, Abbey reached to the table, picked up a pen and notebook and began to write. Simply. She marked the date and without thought wrote in everyday cursive:

> April 28th
>
> Dear Kate,
>
> I know I must have been a brat
>
> sometimes, being the little sister.
>
> But I always looked up to you.
>
> You were strong and sure of everything
>
> and could handle life, it seemed,
>
> with a clear vision and an easy stride.
>
> I admired you. But later things changed
>
> a little, and it made me sad to see.
>
> I miss Katie… Do you?
>
> > Love from,
> >
> > Bee

The words did not sit heavy, nor did they upset Abbey. She leaned back in the recliner again and stared at them awhile, just to be sure.

They felt true, these words. And Bee felt strengthened, having set them to paper. Maybe because it was her sister... the sister who'd been so strong at the core. And so it seemed like strength against strength, meeting her here in the letters; in this truth from long ago.

Abbey smiled. Then she pulled another page free from the notebook and again, jotted the date:

> April 28th
>
> Hi Jeffrey,
>
> Thank you for your letter.
>
> I think I would like to be your friend, too.
>
> $\qquad$ -Abbey

Then she set the pages aside and headed upstairs. A warm bath, Bee told herself, would be reward for this day well done.

Chapter Ten

John Jaffers had been right: thoughts of the writer Ben Cole did, at times, cross Abbey's mind. A part of her did want to spend time with him. He had an intelligence the woman respected, there was a clean honesty about him which sometimes eluded others in his profession... and he was somewhat altruistic, which made Abbey curious and intrigued.

Nonetheless, the woman despised the days when she was forced to call on Ben; ask him to cover this story or that one due to someone else's mistake. —One of her own staffmember's mistakes, she thought, biting at her lip. Today was one of those mismatched days, and just like before Abbey spent only fleeting moments with Ben as she explained the situation. She remained distant -professional- leaving him little opportunity to sight any curiosity or intrigue about her.

For weeks she had slept calmly through a solid six or seven hours. But tonight revisited the dreams. This time, up out of the dreamtime grey, first materialized the little toy bank. On top, the faded metal clown puffed out his cheeks and broke into a tinny laughter. "Unlock the bank," he then uttered. "Unlock the bank to find the treasures all!"

In the dream, Abbey felt frantic. She knew it was important. But there was nothing about to use. In a frenzied motion, she tore at her blouse for the chain around her neck and the key... but it was not there. She dug for her pockets... they were sewn shut.

Then something -a glint of something- caught her eye and she looked up. One of the mobiles from Molly's room hung there, dangling down from nothingness, gently twirling in blues and yellows and pinks... And suddenly a new color spiraled nearby. Bright silver, a thin polished coin flipped down through the mobile and in a single reach, Abbey caught it.

Gasping, she pinched the coin between fingers and lunged for the bank. The clown cackled. "Not silver, I need a penny. I need a penny! I need a penny!"

Abbey swung about again, searching the grey for a sign of something more... but there was nothing.

"-I need a penny! I need a penny! I need-"

And in another single motion, Bee scooped the metal toy into her hand, raised it high and smashed it down. It cracked apart, scattering miniature gears and thick corroded wires, odd metal pieces, and a shower of old coins. Indian heads, wheat pennies and the familiar profiles of Abraham Lincoln... and then the rush of the floodwater, gushing through the dream as it all opened up once more.

The screams came, and Bee found herself drenched but only waist-deep, and she began trudging toward the sound of the voices. There, just ahead. It was her cousin Mackie's voice… and then Brian's… now her old boss from the bank…

And all at once things went silent, except for the ongoing whoosh of the water. Before her now stood a door. It appeared heavy and solid, but Abbey pushed through with hardly an effort, even with the weight of the water all around. And finally, she found her father.

———————————

Another busy week at *Mosaic*; nonetheless Abbey took time to schedule lunch again on Wednesday with Janine. The restaurant they chose was a little bistro. It offered a hip and casual atmosphere but every meal was served in courses, a convenient incentive to spend a full lunch break away from the office.

"So how's the magazine?" Janine began, flapping the linen napkin across her lap.

Abbey rolled her eyes in exaggeration, then explained. "Miscellaneous hectic weeks," she said, "are to be expected with a magazine. I'm just in the mood for a lull, I guess."

And they bantered awhile about work, exchanging insights and gossip, complaints and uncertainties. Just after the salad plates were cleared Abbey told her, "You know, it's so interesting, how every one of us in that office building goes about every day living life: grocery shopping, picking up the kids at daycare, paying bills, having lunch, not having lunch, talking… that's how we spend most of the hours in our days. And yet there's this-" and she stuttered, so unusual, choosing her words, "this other side to things -across some vast river- that we hardly talk about, hardly acknowledge to each other or even to ourselves sometimes. I don't know… these silent dramas we all walk around with." And she breathed a quick inhalation. "Life is weird."

Janine was watching closely. The green of her eyes showed clearly that she understood.

But Abbey went on. "It's not so much taboo as maybe it once was, a few years ago. I mean, it's not that we don't talk about it at all, it's just-" Again she fumbled a bit, but this time fell to quiet.

Janine nodded. "My divorce, for one thing. But I have to keep walking through my days. Do the laundry, tuck Garrett in to bed, wash the car… I have to, Abbey, or honestly I'd lose a year just obsessing about all this and not even realize."

Now the older woman nodded. The waiter brought along their entrées and settled them in with two fresh bottles of sparkling water.

After just a few bites Janine piped, "Well?"

"Hmm?" Anyone who knew Bee's little girl would have seen Molly there in the details of her widened eyes and sudden hint of playfulness.

"So what is your silent drama, Abbey?"

And Bee feigned a sigh, then broke into a broad clear smile. "I like our conversations, Janine," she said quickly. "I'm glad we've gotten to be friends."

Janine let the minute linger, she took a few more bites of her pasta… but she kept an expectant gaze directly across the table to Abbey.

This time, as Bee inhaled, her little sigh was not an exaggeration. She braced herself as she filled her lungs, knowing well that the words she was about to hear reflected back between them would give new form to all the thoughts and ponderings she'd been leaving unnamed these many weeks.

Janine sensed the moment and drew her fork back down to the plate, offering Abbey full attention. Softly, she smiled.

"So," Abbey began, "my mother has Alzheimer's and that's one thing... Truthfully I resent her because I feel like she's taking the easy way out by not remembering; not being able to process so much of this that I can sort a little now that I'm older. And suddenly I *do* want to sort through, whereas before it really didn't interest me or bother me..." She watched Janine's held expression, studying the sincerity there just a little bit more. Then she went on, "I don't like letting myself be vulnerable."

Janine nodded. She picked up her fork again. "I don't really think anybody does, Abbey." And she was surprised, as she went back to another bite of her pasta, that Abbey continued:

"A few months ago, I came across this batch of old letters. Letters I don't remember ever knowing about before. They're all from my childhood -from my Mom, my older sister, friends, a teacher... My 2nd grade teacher, who I hardly even remember, you know? And the letters bring up -I don't know- they point to these things about me, about who I am, that I thought were established and solid. But little sentences in these letters make me question it all, *everything,* and make me wonder what's really me at the core, and what I choose -or chose- maybe even without conscious thought, and what now I ought to choose to let go of. It's… it's all honestly just really weird."

Janine's smile widened.

"My midlife crisis, huh?"

"Oh I think looking at yourself is healthy, Abbey. Some people pick themselves apart in their 20's, some in their 80's, some every New Year's Eve… and some never. But I think it's healthy and, like you said, whether we admit it or not, it goes on every day somewhere in the background. Our silent dramas…"

Abbey nudged her plate of fish aside; she was no longer hungry. "You know, there was this thing between my parents, between me and my sister and brother… It bugs the crap out of me. I used to think it was just the past but something that happened on my birthday last October and now with these letters makes me wonder about that too. It was this thing -not anyone getting punched or bullied or horribly neglected; nobody was a raging alcoholic or dealing with serious depression or anorexia or anything like that. But there was this -this emptiness… some undefined 'something missing' that I worry about now."

Across from her, Janine was a little puzzled.

"I worry that I might pass it down to Molly, and maybe never even see it happen. Do you feel that way sometimes, like there's some odd, intangible disease in your family?…"

Again, the young woman's gaze softened completely. It surprised Bee, the comfort she found there in the subtleties of that expression. Janine began to speak, but Abbey cut her short.

"It's a courageous thing you're doing, Janine. -The divorce. It may be extremely difficult, it may seem unclear, but even for Garrett's sake, the choice you're making now -to seek greater joy- is something of courage. So don't let yourself forget that. Even when he's fourteen years old and pissed at you because of all the years having to live with his parents in two different places…"

A little teary Janine nodded again. "Thanks, Abbey. Thanks." And she set her plate aside too.

For a quick flash of a moment, Abbey thought about the letter this woman might write to her, if years and years in the future she were to come upon it. The words, she imagined, on that evenly folded pastel stationery would be words of peace, she knew. —Words of simple hope and peace. And all at once Abbey felt more at ease than she had in some time.

When the dream came again that night, Abbey's father stood once more at the other side of the doorway. This time, he gestured at her in a slow, heavy, open-handed motion. It was as if he were saying, 'Go back, Abbey Elana. Don't waste your time revisiting this dull place… Go on back and close the door…'

———————————————

The next morning Bee woke with only a misted memory of the doorway, the gesture, and the faded form of her father. But what lingered, as she slipped off her pajamas and headed into the heat of the shower spray, was a jabbing pang of anger.

'A strange turn from yesterday,' she told herself, then continued through the motions of her morning.

There was a meeting at 10am in Edward Endeen's conference room, a small planning meeting to review the progress of goals set in motion back in January. Abbey participated as usual, she thought, with intent and obvious diligence. It seemed however, her supervisor spotted something different. Smoothly, he tidied the dialogue much earlier than usual, and by 10:45 sent everyone else on their way. Yet, pulling Bee aside, he told her, "You've been working hard lately, Abbey. I appreciate your dedication." And he paused a moment, allowing them to exchange an odd lull. His quiet gaze, Bee noticed for the first time, was fleshed out with those little wrinkles here and there that highlighted his particular view of the world... They showed through like an authenticity Abbey hadn't quite considered before when turning thoughts in her head about Edward Endeen.

"Hmm," she muttered spontaneously. Quickly she cleared her throat and added, "Thank you, Ted. I enjoy my position quite a bit."

He nodded, leading in a step toward the door. "Then why not take a long lunch today? Or call it quits early this afternoon? Give yourself some hard-earned perks, Ms. Taft. -You deserve them." And with another nod, he continued down the hall.

Abbey pressed her lips together, wondering.

Whelton Township was an hour and ten minutes from the headquarters of *Mosaic* Women's Magazine. Driving there and driving back... Abbey would miss a lunchtime conference call and return late to her weekly staff meeting. Nonetheless she found herself maneuvering through the parking lot and, with a quick motion, she set the radio to pulse away any second thoughts.

The landscape sparkled with the beauty of full spring, and Whelton itself was simply picturesque. Today Abbey noticed how details were different in the colors of the new season: the great granite stones that made up the bridge over the creek along Main Street, varied in their shapes and hues... the peeling steeple of the Methodist Church, belted with scaffolding and undergoing repair... the mighty oak trees, limbs thick and outstretched over the roadway, spaced four to a block as she drove alongside.

There was a line of traffic and a bustle of pedestrians, now nearing lunchtime. The slowed movement of her car as she edged through town was something Abbey welcomed: it brought even longer pause to sort these fresh sights.

An older man in overalls said a quick hello to Abbey as she met him on the sidewalk. And a young woman and her baby strode by in the sunshine just as Bee rose on her heels up the wide step to the post office. It was different today, to hear voices and to see little transactions taking place inside. 'It all seemed routine enough,' she could hear herself reporting to Greta later, 'people buying stamps and getting packages. Someone needed a money order, I remember. And me... heading over to Box 233 right there near the end of the row... It all seemed so absolutely ordinary.'

And she tugged the key from her necklace and slid it into the lock. As before, it did not turn easily. Abbey jiggled the key just a bit, then tried again. And the door opened.

A strange thought occurred to her just as the key turned: she realized how disappointed and hollow she would feel if the box proved empty this time... But then the little metal and glass door swung open, and she could see the contents revealed.

Sure enough, the box was full again though not crammed to, like before. A fat handful of letters slipped into Bee's grasp and with it, a flurry of feelings rushed through her: the vulnerability, the pitted anxiety, the curiosity, the bewilderment, the heated instinct to flee... And there was something else too, she realized, flashing briefly to the course of warm water over her shoulders, the bubbles and scent of new soap in the shower that morning: A spurt of rage, she felt, firmly gripping the letters and turning away. Rage, and the fired momentum that came with it.

There were sixteen letters this time. Sixteen. Twenty less than last time. Bee sat on a park bench at the center of town, thinking about it. Again, as she considered quantitative details to steady herself, she recalled the strange foreshadow of a thought she'd had when first turning the key this afternoon. 'I'd have felt hollow,' she said aloud, letting her lips and vocal cords actively form the words, announce them, out over the patch of green grass in which she found herself. 'I'd have felt like I was missing out if it had been empty this time...'

And a torrent of notions whipped through her: ponderings, not quite formed, of lost freedom, of ambivalence, of grief, of confusion. Most were fleeting and cascaded through quickly. But one thought turned in on itself somehow, filled itself out into 3-dimensions, brought Abbey to full perception: If the first set of letters had never been there on that early day in March, she herself somehow would have been missing something and yet never would have realized the loss.

Abruptly the woman choked on a gulp of air and coughed a long moment. Her eyes watered, she sputtered and took a tissue from her satchel to wipe at her face. *I would have been missing something, yet never would have realized the loss.* Again, she let the words evolve from thought into sound. It was courageous, she well knew, making them more real that way. And somehow, in noting her courage, Abbey Taft realized she wasn't angry anymore. There was a flicker, and she knew she'd feel it again -but not today.

Raising her gaze, Bee took in the springtime details here too, in the park all around. The hues and shapes in the stretch of varied leaves overhead: spindles, fernlike fingers, swoops, fans and tendrils that fluttered in the breezes... The textures in the stones and the bricks and the bark and the clouds... The delicate sounds of the birds she could barely name and the distant hum of car tires, the insects and the nearly inaudible chorus of trickles and wash from Whelton Creek...

Taking another deep breath, and exhaling clearly this time, she reached back into her satchel and pulled free the new letters. The one to strike her first was tucked in a sage green envelope and was addressed to her in cursive letters. The attached stamp was a washed-out commemorative that pictured an old red stagecoach, rated 25 cents. Inside was a newspaper clipping and a note from her grandmother.

You make us so proud, revealed the note. The handwriting was small and a little jagged, but in a sure hand.

You make us so proud. Your grandpa and I loved

seeing this story about your scholarship, Abbey.

You will do so very well in college and that is

important because you are a talented girl who

deserves to make the most of herself. Your mother

is proud too - she called to tell us all about your

acceptance speech. And your dress is lovely, Dear.

Take care now. Call soon.

Love, G & G

Abbey was quite sure that in days to come there would be tears about this letter. For many reasons. There would be other feelings too, she knew, having read and re-read so many other letters in the weeks gone by. But for now she looked up again at the oak leaves overhead, the color there nearly a match to the paper in her hand, and she watched the breeze flutter through.

Later that week Abbey met Greta and Molly at a t-ball game after work. Bee smiled wide, crossing the field and sighting the mixed dynamics of the game. Nearly chaotic, little boys and girls spurt in dizzy lines around the miniature diamond, parents charging after or shouting directions with broad-armed gestures generally counterclockwise, base to base. Greta was there too, shadowing Molly who was not quite five and one of the smallest little sets of legs on the field. Her thin brown hair peeked just barely under the red baseball cap and her gaze was hard set eyeing second base... but Greta was the one who really caught Abbey's attention. The woman too was alert, watching the next pitch and swing, but her expression was so even somehow; so relaxed. It was as if she soaked in all the details surrounding her -it reminded Bee at once of her afternoon back at Whelton Park. But this was Greta, at a t-ball game for a child who wasn't even her own daughter, well past working hours and with city neighbors she barely knew.

Again it struck Abbey, and later as the three of them took a walk around the bordering meadow, she thanked Greta sincerely.

"Ah, you are welcome, Bee. Thank you for sharing Molly with me."

"Really Greta," Bee continued. "Your caring and dedication are more than I could ever have hoped for. Thank you."

The woman nodded graciously, then looked ahead to watch as Molly swung on a low tree branch.

"So what would you be doing tonight if you weren't here with us? Are things going well with James -isn't that who you've been seeing?"

"Yeah," she said, though with little enthusiasm. "Things with James are fine. He plays trumpet you know, in a little band at some of the clubs. He's trying to get me to sing..." Her deep brown eyes sparkled now, remarking about it. "I'm not much of a singer, Bee, you know that." And she giggled, crooning a few notes out over the pasture. Up ahead, Molly cocked her head and laughed along with them.

"But it's fun," Greta went on. "-Becoming a regular at the clubs. I like meeting people, all sorts."

"You are such an observer," Abbey told her. "It's intimidating to some of the rest of us..." She grinned, then patted Greta's shoulder.

Expression softening, Greta noted the gesture.

"See?" Abbey said. "You notice every damn thing, and all the implications... You ought to write a book."

And with that the nanny's gaze shifted again, this time crooking into an angled smirk. Smug, she taunted, "How do you know I'm not?"

After a chuckle Bee told her outright, "You look like a pirate with that expression. Or like Robin Hood. A well-intended, virtuous land-pirate, Greta Duvall."

And there was a pause as Molly stooped to gather a handful of wildflowers, calling to them to help her name all the blossoms.

"Dandelion, cherry blossoms, lavender I think," Abbey recited. "And..." She and Molly both looked to Greta for the name of the little purplish one, somehow star-like and obvious there in the bouquet.

"Periwinkle," Greta revealed, smiling as Bee scooped up the little girl and gave her a kiss.

"See, we have a lot to learn from Greta, don't we Molly?" And the child bubbled into laughter as her mother tickled her ribs. Wriggling, she fought herself free and dashed off for more flowers.

After awhile Bee told Greta she had been writing a few replies to some of the letters. "I'm wondering if I should take them to the post office box, see if they mysteriously get mailed off..."

"Maybe mailing them isn't the point."

Without much thought Bee returned, "Maybe holding on to them isn't either."

Greta nodded, obviously impressed. "Great insight, Abbey. I'm really proud of you." And she patted Bee on the shoulder, mirroring her friend's earlier show of tenderness.

———————————

The next morning plummeted Bee into a series of minor disasters at the office. A missed deadline, a loose succession of thin excuses, one complaint from Endeen and two more from her staff... "What in the world does your annual physical at the doctor's office have to do with my monthly report?!" she found herself barking to one of her assistants, even before noon. The young woman apologized, but the look in her eyes read something different.

Abbey glanced back to the demographics update she'd been skimming. -Something about the accompanying memo from Edward made her throw the whole thing into the recycle bin: *Up the word count on the Entertainment News, and not just for the summer issues... We need at least two minor articles a month on the celeb/s, trends and hype.*

When she picked up the phone to buzz Sam Beauregard, only to find he was out sick today, she finally allowed herself to droop into her chair and wheeze a deep, slow shrug. It evolved into a mutter of curses, and she stared long out the window.

She picked up Molly at her friend's house that evening, and they went out to the diner for burgers and milkshakes. Later, after a warm bath,

Abbey still felt as if her day had been virtually non-productive; with a fresh glass of port in hand she nestled into the recliner and opened one of the new envelopes. Here, she was sure, there was work to be done.

Abruptly she paused, fingers just barely under the crease of paper. "...Not so much work," she found herself saying aloud. "-Substance." And with a ginger, more mindful motion, she guided the letter open and soaked in the inkstrokes that aligned themselves there before her.

> You were born too late to burn your bra,
> Abbey. (I was too, by the way.)
> Why don't you just get real and stop
> making Mom and Dad mad? Everyone
> would be happier, including you.
>
> Kate

Abbey felt a little twinge, then began to laugh. It was no wonder, she told herself, if these were the thoughts jostling through her older sister's head, that she and Kate never seemed compatible. Kate would have been sixteen at the time, Abbey barely a teenager. Indeed, it was funny.

Sipping at the port, Bee wondered what she'd done at twelve or thirteen to anger her parents. It hadn't taken much to displease her mother, certainly, but to elicit anger? She could faintly recall snapshots of explosive moments with her father: once when she'd whined about sharing a room with Kate... once at someone's birthday party... once the weekend Grandpa had died. There was a foggy notion of tension, winding with the clockhands as the afternoon set in on Sundays; greyed, hazy visions of herself keeping eyes wide and mouth pinched as twilight closed in. But there was nothing more.

Maybe Kate was simply referring to their mother's general dissatisfaction with her children. In her constant striving for the best from them, Caroline Taft left little room for much that resembled utter contentment. There was rarely the passion of anger either, as Abbey recalled. Sipping again at her drink, she came to wonder if Kate, perhaps, had a different perspective.

In her three extra years was there some other wisdom? As the eldest, had she seen a progression unfold that young Abbey had simply never noticed? It had not really occurred to Bee before. And, knowing Kate as she did, it was tempting to dismiss the idea altogether: Kate's particular outlook seemed more skewed than wise... Nonetheless, she set the letter on the end table, where she would read it again later.

The port was thick and sweet on Abbey's tongue. Savoring it, she was brought to realize that the complex mix of sensations highlighted just how tasteless her hours earlier in the day had been. With a deliberate motion she reached for another letter.

> Abbey,
> We never had a doubt that you'd go to
> college and graduate school and be successful.
> Choosing to major in Business is interesting,
> I'm sure, but something a bit more specific
> would seem the stronger position. You've

always liked the scales of balance and

justice - why not be an attorney? Even

better, why not be a judge?

-Mom

This information was not new. Many times, her mother had pressured Abbey about the details of her schooling and her career. Her father, too, had been involved on occasion. And for the most part, though not then easy, Bee had thought their assertions and guidance had been a good thing: over-zealous, a little harsh maybe, but support nonetheless. With Kate, she remembered, they had urged her toward nursing, then kept rather quiet the next four years as their oldest daughter went on her way. Never the same pressure because by then Kate -well past Katie, certainly- had long established her own sights for herself. Not that nursing wasn't a solid and lofty goal in and of itself. But in Caroline and Donald Taft's opinion, it clearly wasn't *doctoring*.

Yet something else struck Abbey tonight. This letter was deeply creased and wrinkled; the paper softened extensively. It was as if the page had been crumpled once into a wad and Bee had to wonder: Had it been her father, tired of her mother's ongoing expectations?... Had it been Kate, having mistakenly happened upon the letter, in jealousy who had balled it up to throw it away?... or had it been Caroline herself? And the port shuddered in the glass as Abbey wondered... Had her mother, at some point, considered giving up on her?

There was a flash all at once of emotions again through Abbey Taft; the wine glass barely made it back to the table. -A jolt of rage, a skitter of fine bewilderment, a floundering of sadness, a wrench of envy, a spatter of sheer giddiness, a stabbing of jagged guilt, a sudden lull and that hollowness she couldn't quite define.

'Why is it that a crumpled damn piece of paper can make me feel like I'm spinning out of control toward a cliff?' she could hear herself saying.

whynotbeajudge??

She winced and chuckled and sputtered all at once, grabbing for the port again as if it would steady her somewhat.

'Hey,' came a tender echo, Greta's echo, floating in… 'You have a past. Just like the rest of us. These words might make you feel vulnerable but they're not bad. They're fine, you know? They're amazing, but they're just words and letters.'

With a gulp, Abbey drank the rest of the port heavily down.

Work at the office was little different the next day. Abbey felt as if she was making no discernible headway again midst the ongoing lurches and twists of another series of excuses, errors and lethargy. Well before noon she dialed Ben Cole's number and this time the motion did not make her feel uneasy. 'I'm well past that,' she told herself, thinking of the letters from the previous night. Today, instead, the prospect of spending a little time with the freelance writer seemed invigorating.

Ben had been available for an afternoon meeting; Abbey had pretended her day's schedule was too full. Instead, she'd decided, an evening at the pub seemed a better chance at breaking out of this strange cycle of thin productivity. Finally, as she hung up the phone, the woman had the sense she was regaining a modicum of control.

His brown eyes were deep, soft, captivating. Not like the piercing brown of so many other acquaintances and lovers she'd sighted. Ben's invited closeness; Ben's portrayed calm.

"So nice to see you, Abbey," he smiled, reaching like he always did for her extended hand.

She shook, a little less stiffly perhaps, and perched on the barstool beside him. Gesturing to the bartender, Ben knowingly ordered her a gin and tonic. It brought her to a smile. "You know," she admitted, facing him, "you're a dependable boat in the storm, Ben. I can always count on you, no matter the forecast. Thanks for that."

He raised a brow, obviously surprised at her words. Not so much that she complimented him; more that she chose to take the time to do so. He adjusted a little more comfortably onto the stool. "I appreciate the work, Abbey," he said. "You know that. And I like *Mosaic* – a balance of quality editorial and marketability… It's respectful of its readers. When it comes to magazines for women, that's not easy to pull off. So, thank *you*." And he toasted her, curving his mouth to let her know he was well-aware that she, herself, had much to do with the magazine's integrity and ongoing success.

She took a sip, then breathed deep. The man was indeed attractive. And he sat, silently, watching her. Undoubtedly he awaited her plunge into the dry details of the assignment.

Coyly, Bee licked the lingering sting of alcohol from her lips. Then quickly she told him, "I have two stories for you, Ben. My staff has been useless this week and I'm just ready to move on. But I'm going to email you the spec/s tomorrow, first thing, all right? Let's just take this evening to chat a little..."

His smile widened, just a bit, and he toasted her again. She considered waiting him out, to discover what tact he might take at this new opportunity. But then she thought better of it and spoke first. "Tell me again about the travel book you're working on? It sounded refreshing."

He spun the details into an ebb and pull of sentences, lyrical, like a storyteller. The book was about hidden vacation treasures sprinkled throughout North America. Easy to get to, affordable to visit, memorable and unique... The rhythm of his voice drew her in even more than the details themselves. Then her gaze wandered to the hue of his eyes again, and the sound of his voice faded a little. Captivating... Inviting... With a blink Abbey looked away.

There was a pause, and she suddenly realized he'd stopped talking. This time she let the moment to itself, and shortly, Ben put to her, "So, you're enjoying the springtime? Any big plans for this summer?"

She shook her head over the rim of her glass. "Molly and I -my daughter- went on a family cruise a few months ago. It was terrific. This summer, I'm not sure. Maybe just a long weekend at the beach..."

He refrained from suggesting a travel spot from the book. Perfect, Abbey thought, watching him again. And she ordered another drink.

They decided on hors d'ouevres, and Ben asked for a story or two about Molly. Proudly she indulged, the food arrived and their conversation turned to a comment or two about Edward Endeen. Ben wondered about Sam Beauregard and some of the other staff he knew;

briefly Abbey described the low points of her week.

"Ah, that's the cycle, Abbey," he told her evenly. "The life cycle of Fulfillment just goes that way." Then he added, "Well, maybe 'fulfillment's' not the word. 'Aspiration…' 'Success…' 'Productivity…' Somewhere in between, professionally, there is that word. Anyway, it'll come back around -that's just how it goes."

Abbey wasn't sure if it was the glide of the gin, but something about the deep brown of this man's eyes went well past captivating and abruptly reminded her of the gritty wisdom of Greta Duvall. A last nibble of a tortilla chip and Bee stood to go.

Ben had not pressed his way any closer to her all evening, but now he reached for her forearm. Smiling again, he put to her, "Where do you think you're going? It's early, I'd love to talk some more-" And he said her name, it slid from his lips so smoothly… drawn out so that the sound of the two syllables lingered…

Bee offered a broad smile and flatly set a twenty dollar bill on the bar. Then she turned and left.

At home she paid the babysitter, checked in on the sleeping Molly and headed quickly for the coffeemaker in the kitchen. It took less than three minutes for Abbey to settle herself with a large mug of steaming coffee and cream back in her recliner, shoes tossed aside, with a new letter in hand. As a flash of Ben's face crossed her mind, the woman quickly slid her thumb under the envelope, and tugged the letter free. And there on dulled notebook paper was the spirited cursive lettering of a young John Jaffers.

Chapter Eleven

"I must have been what, 27?" he was saying. His brow was furrowed. His gaze was dark; perplexed. Shoulders low, hands open there over the table. He was looking up at the woman with everything about him passive. He'd offered up his self-defense.

"Read it out loud." Her words were nearly a hiss. It startled him.

"Abbey, Sweetheart, sit down." And John rose a little from his chair to coax her.

With a sigh she acquiesced. Finally, the rattles and pings of the café chimed and registered in her ears again… John Jaffers relaxed a little as he saw her draw a full breath.

"Now what's this all about, Abbey?" he asked, tone utterly sweet and concerned. He held the letter, but stared over it to keep his eyes on Bee.

"Read. Read it aloud."

He could tell she would say nothing further. "Well at least you're calmer," he nodded, and flicked the page a bit in the early morning sunlight that beamed through the windows. With a squint, he cleared his throat and began:

> I am not sure there's such a thing as bisexual, Abbey...
> Why don't you make up your mind and commit?
> You and I kissed – so what? It doesn't mean we
> have to be engaged. So go ahead, make up your mind.
> I don't care what the end result is, I just want you to
> make the damn decision. I'd really like to know,
> *really,* what it is you want before we go any further
> together with this friendship. More than that,
> I'd like to know -really- *that you know what it is*
> *that you want.*
>
> -John Jaffers

"What does it mean?" Again, nearly a hiss.

"W-well-" He let the page dip toward the table, facing her again. Then he went suddenly quizzical. "Where did you get this? I really don't remember ever writing you a letter like this..."

"What does it mean, John?"

He was silent, quite a while. Then he sipped at his morning tea, made a face as it had gone cold. As he reached to summon the waitress, Abbey gripped his hand.

"I never read it before. But I've found it now, and it pisses me off. Who were you to judge me, who were you to-"

"Wait." And he turned his wrist so as to take her hand in his own. "I was 27, I was barely aware of- No. Abbey, Sweetie, ask me what I think about things now. Ask me what I have to say about you and commitment now... About your ability to take the reins now. That's what pisses you off."

"How dare you." And her face went bleak. It was a hard-edged look, well-practiced from her years in business management. It hid the hollowness, but John knew better.

"I'd never be judging you Bee, you know that. It would just be my opinion -one cocky young boy's opinion, who'd never been well-kissed before you came into my life. C'mon, it's *me*..."

Again, his tone was utterly genuine and concerned. He massaged her fingers, watchful as her expression evolved. There was a hint of calm now, a subtle hint... He could see it in the nuances of the upswing of her eyebrow, the changing flecks of grey in her irises as they went from fire to ash...

This time he whispered to her. "I know that you know what you want, Abbey. Maybe I was just upset it wasn't me. It broke my heart a little..." Bee blinked and looked down to where he gently caressed her hand. He continued, "People generally inflict the severest wounds on each other out of hurt or fear, you know that. I was hurt, Sweetie."

She focused on his motions over her fingertips, blinked again, staring hard to keep her gaze averted from his own. –She wasn't at all sure she believed the words he had offered... but the sound of them soothed her. And for now, that seemed to make a difference.

Later that morning at work, Bee emailed the assignments to Ben Cole. She included mild pleasantries, well aware that a higher level of personability was warranted… but she couldn't bring herself to it.

'Ben is kind and interesting and available,' she could hear repeating through her day. At first, she assumed such whispered insights to be reflections somehow of Greta's clear thinking, but at some point after lunchtime she realized that no, the voice she imagined held a timbre more like Catherine's. '…and he scares you,' the hazy flow continued.

'As if that isn't obvious,' Abbey scrawled in a rugged slant across her notepad. And before she slammed herself out the door and into an afternoon staff meeting, she added more:

~~'This ongoing conversation with myself wears me thin.'~~

'This ongoing conversation with myself fires me to new passion.'

By four o'clock that afternoon Bee was feeling feverish; by seven she was shaky with chills and sat bundled in a heavy quilt before the television. Molly poked at her now and then. Sweetly, she piped, "Mommy, you okay?" And they both spent the night on the couch, t.v. droning.

On Saturday Abbey managed to call a neighbor, who was happy to take Molly for several hours and returned with a thermos full of chicken soup. After a quick but sincere thank-you, Bee retreated again to the living room, her daughter in tow. The two cuddled on the couch once more for several hours of kids' videos. Molly giggled and chattered and eventually toted a box of cereal out to the coffeetable; Abbey smiled at the little girl and, for the most part, dozed. The weekend ebbed into a timeless blur.

"Abbey. Bee?" The urgent coaxing filtered through the black lull of her fevered sleep and eventually the woman wakened. It was Greta who faced her, kneeling at the recliner, waving a thermometer almost immediately as Bee opened her eyes.

"Molly says you haven't moved all weekend. She's scared, Bee. *Why didn't you call me??*"

The woman managed a lopsided grin, her cheeks flushed and damp. "I moved. Got up from the couch and made it all the way over here…" And she tapped weakly at the armrest of her chair.

"Hush," Greta snapped, popping the thermometer into Bee's mouth. "I called your office, so that's squared away. And Molly's getting dressed. Once she sees you're awake and all right, I'll drive her to school. -It's already 9:15."

Abbey was a little surprised, but didn't have the strength to show it beyond a raised brow. The thermometer beeped.

"One o' two point two." Greta scowled. Then she offered a comforting smile instead, and headed off to retrieve some medicine.

It proved to be a fitful morning. Bee was in and out of a heavy sleep, her fever raging. Greta alternated ibuprofen and a fever reducer, barely managing the temperature at 102.5. She had her hand on the telephone to call the doctor, then a thought struck her suddenly and she withdrew. With a tray –soup, crackers, orange slices and ginger ale– she went and sat next to Abbey.

"Bee," she called, rocking the woman with a firm grip at her shoulder. "Bee, Honey, wake up-"

"Unnhh…" And she rolled her head and attempted to curl in on herself for more sleep.

"Abbey." Greta shook the recliner a bit. "Tell me what you did Friday. Before you got sick. Was it a good day at work? Were you thinking about the letters?... Abbey."

A little more nudging, a moment's wading through various mumbles as Abbey slowly became more coherent, and finally Greta got an answer.

"Ben. Ben Cole. Nnn- I saw John that morning. Breakfast. He's a snob about his goddamn tea."

Greta prodded further, her insight proving infallible. "John wrote you a letter, didn't he? What did it say?"

"Oh that he's a goddamn coward- No, he called *me* a goddamn coward," she slurred. "And indecisive." Her eyes flashed, fully awake, and she reached for the ginger ale.

"John knows you really well," Greta ventured. "Maybe he was right. Maybe fifteen years ago you were indecisive."

There was not another flash, but Abbey rolled a dark gaze in Greta's direction. "He was judging me," she said, breath heavy. "And he didn't say it to my face." Again, she sucked at the straw of her soda.

Greta tempted her with an orange slice, offering a soft and compassionate stare. But her words came blunt once again. "So why are you so angry at your mother, Abbey?"

"What are you, my therapist now? I'm gonna have to pay you a higher… hourly… rate," she managed, again out of breath.

Greta pulled a rocking chair close alongside, and sat down next to her friend. "I'm actually serious, Bee. Are you mad at your Mom for the way things are now, or is this from the past... or is it that you don't know or is it a mix or...?"

"Why- why do we have to figure this out now?"

"It's why you're sick, Bee. Your body is dealing with all this, burning it out -it's good... It's all good, but it's just that if we can unravel some of the feelings well, then your fever will pass. You'll feel better." And her own tone changed, noticeably.

"You'll feel better..." The brown of her eyes was a light chocolate, Bee suddenly noticed. It was a soft and soothing color, something to drink in. Sometimes intriguing. Mostly intimidating. Perhaps that was the reason Bee usually kept a certain distance in facing the woman; perhaps it was why she hadn't quite noticed the hue before now.

Greta offered another piece of the orange. Abbey took it and smiled. She drank a little soup, nibbled at a cracker. Neither spoke for several minutes. Then Bee cleared her throat definitively and said, "Okay but after this -after I'm better- I want to hear some really juicy stories about your family history, Ms. Duvall." And she smirked, pausing, then grew more serious. Taking a full breath she added, "Why don't you read me the letters, Greta? Some of them? One at a time."

Greta smiled at her, nodding. She went and gathered the stack of letters and began. Her voice was solid, but somewhat quiet, and she paused but a short moment between each one:

Ms. Taft:

You have an excellent mind

and strong communication style.

I would easily recommend you to

a doctoral program, should you

decide to pursue it.

-Professor Z. Marcos

Bee-

You piss me off, Woman!

You're so damn perfect:

smart, sexy, driven.

You create your own luck

and doors open

and here you are, balancing it all.

If I didn't love you so much,

I'd HATE you!!

-Laurie

(the peon roommate who pays

half your rent)

Abbey,

The day we met, my

heart skipped a beat.

I adore you.

-Unsigned

Congratulations, Abbey! We are very proud

of your graduation cum laude. Your mother

and dad are proud as well. We all look forward

to watching your successes multiply these

next few years. Now, enough school for awhile…

Any wedding bells in the distance??

Love, G & G

I miss you, Bee.

Here, alone with Mom

is kind of -well-

different. Have fun

this summer.

Love, Cale

Abbey,

You've achieved a certain

independence, which allows

for genuine opportunities.

Don't squander the moments

ahead. These years of post-graduate

work are important too. We're

all behind you.

-Mom

My baby boy is a joy, Abbey;

I can't wait for you to meet him.

Motherhood is just the right fit

for me, I love it! Make time to visit

us soon.

Kate

Abruptly Greta did some shuffling, and added in a few of the older letters as well:

B.

You're so boring.

You don't care about anything and you're

not too deep, not too shallow. High school

is about exploration: You're sidestepping.

Is it fear? Low esteem? A control trip?

Arrogance?

-I don't care anymore.

Have a great life.

-S.T.

By the way, here's a poem for you-

When I was born,

my eyes were bright and glowing

with the anticipation of sheer possibility.

Today my gaze is greyed;

dimmed with time and loss.

I am not a stone, like some of the others,

but I am changed.

Greta glanced up at the recliner. Abbey was relaxed, but her face was tight; contemplative. Without the buffering daze of the fever, Greta thought, she might have been crying at hearing such words. There was a long moment of silence between them.

"You know, Greta, listening to you read them out loud is different. It hits me in a new way, the tone and rhythm of each message. Thank you."

Greta smiled to her again, tenderly. Then she offered, "Finding yourself can be relatively easy, Bee. Letting it go is the challenge."

Abbey exaggerated a grin, her cheeks flushed once again. Greta could tell just by looking at her that the fever had spiked. "Here," she continued, "give me your hand."

Without much consideration, Bee reached. Greta grasped her fingers and closed them into a fist, holding tight. "Now, try to open."

Abbey pushed against her, but it wasn't easy. With a second try, she finally managed to force Greta's grip.

"Again," her friend said, pushing back once more. "A fist -you've found yourself. Like a shell, self-contained, well-understood, well-defined... Now, break free. Let it go. Open to the undefined, the unknown, the something-more."

Abbey forced her fingers out of the clench, casting off Greta's hand entirely with the effort. A drop of sweat etched itself down her temple. A tear did the same, slow and heavy, down the frame of her reddened cheek.

That night Greta slept in the guest room, insisting on reassuring Molly with a return to the familiar schedule. She managed to coax Abbey into a dinner of pretzel sticks and applesauce, then walked her up to bed, dabbing a wet cloth at her forehead before Bee fell into another deep sleep.

It was strained tonight however, and Bee tossed and twisted herself under a tangle of blankets. Faces materialized in and out of her dreams -features forming at random out of the grey. Each one a letter writer, they appeared ghostly and haunting, disturbing the flow of her slumber. They would not speak, would not hover long, but simply ebbed into silent form and then retreated. One after another, and again.

Ultimately, a dream realization came to her, foggy and slow. Charged with weightedness and a strange soundless momentum -like the coming of far distant thunder, like a throbbing, tidal undercurrent- it crept into being and made itself known to her. And in her sleep, to be forgotten by the dawn, Abbey screamed. 'Where are you?! Where are you?!' Face after face, misted feature after hazy form, and not one of them had been her father.

By Tuesday afternoon Bee was pink with a healthier color, and felt strong enough to shower. When Molly came home from preschool and her dance class, Bee gave her a hug and thanked the little girl for her care and patience the past few days. They played several rounds of Go-Fish, then Abbey retreated once more for a nap.

She considered pushing herself to return to work the next day but couldn't envision successfully broaching the subject with Greta. So instead, Bee slept in, allowed herself to sit quietly and watch the light through the windows change as the day lengthened, and she eased herself into letting thoughts flow about the letters. It was a simple series of hours.

Work the remainder of the week was busy but non-eventful somehow. The pace was fast and the hours were full, but not hectic. Abbey accomplished everything she needed to, and went home for the weekend relaxed and rather revitalized.

————————————————

"Well, what does the stick say, Molly?"

The girl wiped her thumb over a smudge at the end of her tiny wooden signpost. "Looks like green puffy things, Mommy," she reported. "With a 'L.'"

"L… Hmm… Lo-Lo-Lollipops? La-La-Lambs? La-La-Lilacs? Lizards? Lemons?"

"No, Mommy! Something that grows in the garden. Like a bean or a carrot."

"Oh, something for our salad? Like broccoli or onions or tomatoes?"

"No!" squeaked Molly, a little flustered. But she set herself to thinking.

Bee watched as the child's tongue held there, just behind her top front teeth, coaxing the initial sound and the full word that would follow. Moments passed… then Molly's blue eyes sparkled. "Lettuce!" she triumphed.

"Oh yeah," Abbey smiled. "That's kind of like a green puffy thing. See, you were right all along, Molli-pop."

The little gardener rolled her eyes, then crouched next to her mother to see just which new stems poking through the musty dirt were weeds. Soon enough, she was tugging with care to tend her rows of new lettuce.

The sun was warm, and Bee and Molly took several breaks to sip at lemonade tea and lounge in the patio chairs. They played more Go-Fish and after lunch Bee donned her wide brimmed straw hat and set up the sprinkler for Molly to run through. By mid-afternoon they retreated back inside and found themselves dozing on the couch together once again.

Just as she slipped quietly into sleep it occurred to Abbey: she couldn't manage them frequently as her nature was too extroverted or too manic or too mature or too responsible or too superficial, somehow- but these were the days that bordered on perfect. And her sleep was filled with ease, through and through.

"Gramma, Gramma!" blurted Molly Taft, skipping with a singsong voice as she hurried across the room. Four or five elderly residents looked up and beamed, hearing the call. But none of them was Caroline.

Such didn't sadden Abbey today but it did occur to her how these things were framing her little girl's perceptions of her grandmother. Had Molly been born five or ten years earlier, the experience would have been very different. For all of them. Today, it was a notion to ponder, at least for a few moments, as she and Molly shuffled in and said their hellos.

"Gramma," Molly went on brightly, "my lettuce plants in the garden are growing and growing. I weeded yesterday and maybe next weekend we'll have a salad!" And she glanced at Abbey, grinning.

"Well, if the bunny doesn't come back and munch it all!"

Caroline stared at the little girl, and a curve made its way across her set expression.

"We're so lucky to have Molly, aren't we, Mom?" Bee said, squeezing gently at her daughter's shoulder. Molly beamed again.

Set before Caroline was a small jigsaw puzzle; she turned back to it and Molly leaned in to help as she could. A caregiver wandered by with chilled apple juice. After several minutes Abbey asked again if her mother recalled when she'd taken singing lessons, but today the older woman didn't offer a reply.

"Was this morning a pancake breakfast?" she asked instead. "It's Sunday, must've been french toast or pancakes..."

"Mmm-" Molly licked her lips.

"Mom? Were the pancakes with blueberries today?"

Caroline kept her eyes on the puzzle. "Peaches on the side," she muttered. "Coffee, black. Maple syrup and butter. Egg over-easy. Bacon. Juice, rancid."

Abbey pressed her lips together and coaxed a smile, although no one particularly noticed. Molly cheered as her grandma locked a new piece into place in the lake scene spread before them.

"Well, the coffee's the important part of breakfast anyway," Bee went on, gaze drifting. She was surprised when her mother answered quickly:

"Indeed."

And the two exchanged a glance. Abbey broke into a spontaneous chuckle. It was good, she realized, to sit here across from her mother with less tension; less sadness; less frustration.

'Accepting someone -even your mother- where she is right here, right now, despite the past, despite the future, that's a gift,' came the voice in her head. Today she was unsure whether it was Greta's, Catherine's, or someone else's entirely. Nonetheless, it was her mother here who was offering the backdrop for the insight.

"Thanks, Mom," Bee said quietly. And this time, both Molly and Caroline looked up to face her. Together, all three shared a tender moment.

As she and Molly drove home that afternoon, Abbey turned on the radio -an upbeat, light rhythm to match her newfound mood. She watched the hue of the open sky and let her mind clear, thoughts wandering with little intensity. Consciously inhaling a deep breath, Bee noted just how relaxed she felt, and commended herself.

After awhile, Molly fell asleep in the backseat. Bee turned off the music and instead allowed herself to soak in the silence. And abruptly she squealed on the brakes, jolting with a new realization. The car veered, smacking with a lurch into the curb. Reeling, Abbey checked on Molly, who was still fast asleep, breath even.

Another deep inhalation -this time to steady herself- and Abbey maneuvered the car down the road.

:Her mother was utterly present today, as she was everyday these past few years. It was different, very different, than when Bee had been a child or a young adult... but even then, Caroline Taft had been involved. She'd been dependable; she'd been a constant.

Abbey's father, she suddenly realized, had not been the same. She had idolized the man, she had remembered him with such gentle fondness… and yet his place in her world had been uneven. Sporadic. At times he was there, yet somehow invisible. At other times, as she now looked back, Abbey couldn't even recall her father's place in the house at all. –His chair at the dinner table, empty. –His coat over the banister, missing.

And not once… it occurred to Abbey now… not once, had he written her a letter.

As she lay in bed later that night, Bee had a faint recollection of screaming at her father at some point, maybe twice, midst the foggy landscape of her dreams. Intuitively, she was sure it had been cathartic… though she was just as sure there was more to be exchanged between them.

For now, there were no tears. There was no flash of red before her eyes, no hollow in her belly. Somehow, the absence of such flares reassured her. But words came, and sounded themselves on her lips there in the moonlight as the late darkness of the night settled in.

"You had things to teach me too," she said softly and with deliberateness. "I wish you hadn't given up on yourself, on us…"

And there was a pause, though the moonlight remained. Then Bee continued, a little quieter still:

"You have things to teach me, Daddy. Don't give up on me. Don't give up on me now…"

For several days thereafter, Abbey was unusually quiet. She was not heavy, nor distracted nor sullen… she was simply taking in more of the silence, and allowing it time, as needed, to soak into her very cells. That stillness somehow seemed necessary.

Abbey was not one who organically understood such things, or usually considered them to be an integral part of herself, but this she did not question. Not for a moment. And those around her did not either, which was somehow reassuring as well. Even Molly somehow slowed her pace to match her mother's, and Greta too refrained from remarking about the change.

About a week later, however, as Abbey was slipping back into her routine, Greta invited herself to stay for dinner. She cooked flavorful veggie burgers, fresh corn on the cob and homemade onion rings. Molly bubbled with laughter. The table was bright and alive; the yellow corn kernels burst with each bite and the smell of the fry-grease and mixed herbs lingered, well through the meal. Everything was cheerful and light, but for the brief moment Greta made mention:

"Abbey," she said, with a clear purposefulness in her eyes, "You can be proud of the relationships you're creating for yourself… With your mother, with Janine, even with me. With Molly-" And she gave a sidewards glance, somehow hearkening back to the mysterious words the psychic had uttered nine months prior.

There was a twinge as she verbalized it, and Abbey knew how

meaningful her point was. "What a good friend you are," Bee thought to say, and the evening returned to laughter.

Later that night, Bee found herself alone once more with the letters, surrounded by darkness and the fragrant warmth of a cup of herbal tea. The evening had closed in around her, like so many other recent nights... It brought the woman to a smile. Indeed, she thought, Greta was right. And Abbey took a moment to rejoice in this new facet of herself, this precious time she continued to spend in reflection... this new companionship she felt with the silence. Truly, Bee could take notice of herself growing. It was a satisfying achievement indeed.

With that, she set the letters aside and instead took up her pen.

> 'Dear Bee,' she began, 'Last year my birthday really did mark a new beginning. It's worn me down, frustrated me, brought me to tears... but it really has been growth. And I'm seeing that there's another level to intimacy, that before I'd been too afraid of, or too busy for, or too arrogant about... And the view, I'm realizing, is just beautiful. And amazing. There's an intimacy within myself that's been missing before. And there's something about offering that to others, so that they're not left empty somehow after an interaction, but instead they're nourished... I don't know, exactly. But it's an important step beyond selfishness, for me, and into this new plane of intimacy that I'm -frankly- just learning about.'

As she continued, Bee took a breath, filling her lungs and sorting thoughts as she pieced together the last sentences, saying them out loud with the motion of the pen.

'I'm grateful to myself, for this. I've really come to a place where I'm able to acknowledge that.'

And she signed it, hand firm as she looped the familiar series of letters:

'Love from Abbey'

"Here, Sweetheart," she said, helping to hold the collection of papers tight as the little girl crisscrossed the pastel pink ribbon over and through. "And this way, Molly, for the top."

Together, they fastened the batch of letters tidily, with a finishing bow. With a lavender ribbon, they tied the second set as well, and with yellow, the stack of reply letters that Bee had written. The note to herself remained separate, and Abbey stored them all in the old cigar box until the day came when she was ready to make another trip to Whelton.

A week or so later when the day arrived, it was a misty afternoon and alone Bee drove through the quaint neighborhoods and made her way to the little post office. With the single letter to herself in hand, she went inside and jiggled the stubborn key in Box 233.

Within, to her surprise, were no more letters. Instead, there was a very small ornate box. Abbey gasped a little, a twinge skittering through reminiscent of the first time she'd made her discovery here. The worn box, adorned with tiny crystals and raised, rustic metalwork, felt weighted in her hand. She opened it with a tiny click of the inner latch, entirely unsure what she might find.

-It was a locket, tarnished... imperfect... smudged and sunken on one edge with a small dent. Abbey's finger trembled as she ran a touch over the little circle of gold -it was so familiar and yet so foreign somehow. Like an ancient lullaby she could faintly recall, but not quite.

Time ebbed as she worked up the conviction to open the hinge and see what was inside. But the locket was empty, except for the inscribed letter on the front face. In old world script, etched with boldness by a careful hand, was the letter "B."

Abbey felt herself spin; she leaned on the bank of postal boxes and again took a deep inhalation. As always when she visited this place, she had the unrelenting urge to reel around the counters, catch sight of anyone who had a look in their eyes disclosing that they were somehow involved in this mystical exchange. As always, there was no one.

She slipped the letter to herself into Box 233, almost clumsily, then closed the little door and headed away.

Back at the car, again taking time to finger the worn locket, Abbey allowed herself several minutes of sheer disbelief, of undefined puzzlement, of outright dizziness.

This was a whole new level.

Chapter Twelve

Greta's expression was priceless, as she ran a gentle finger over the circular locket, gauging time back to the craftsman who'd inscribed it... and to his client, who had requested the particular letter. For the first time, her eyes flashed well beyond the usual caring and tenderness she'd expressed these many months about this quiet mystery. Even she, Abbey could tell, was having trouble digesting the appearance of this little piece of worked gold, and its inherent message.

"Wow," the nanny mouthed. "It's remarkable, Abbey. I-I really can't imagine how this is all happening. It's beyond words, really." And she looked up from the locket, donning a more familiar smile. "I wonder whose pictures belong in here?"

Abbey shrugged her shoulders, not even guessing. "I called the post office. The postmaster said the box has been rented under the name of Taft for at least 3 years. I asked if there was a record of payment or something -he says no, which means it was probably always just paid with cash."

"Did you ask how long into the future it's rented?" Greta questioned.

"Apparently for another 7 years. And the addressee on file is me; no one else is listed… Weird," Bee said with a heavy beat. Seated in the recliner, her shoulders were hunched somehow and she looked a little defeated. "It's getting a little too weird suddenly, Greta," she admitted. "I think I'd settled into the letters, I was getting something out of that situation, I was handling it. This locket is beautiful," she smiled, fingering the little trinket. "It's simple and it really seems like a special keepsake… but it's throwing my equilibrium like a ton of bricks. I don't know," she ended, flushing a little and rubbing her cheek. "Maybe I should be calling the police or something…"

"Well," Greta offered, sitting down beside her, "the letters may be inexplicable too, but we know they've been a gift. I'm going to bet this locket will be too."

The women exchanged a long stare. Then Greta continued, "We can be bewildered about how it's all happened, sure… That's natural, I'd say. But ultimately, we can dismiss it as too crazy or we can trust it… Somehow, some way, we can make the decision to trust it. And go from there. I think that's what you'll do, Abbey. –That's what you did with the letters."

As she'd done several times in recent weeks, Greta reached for Bee's hand, clasped and squeezed just slightly in affirmation. It secured her balance somewhat, and Abbey was brought to close her eyes and sit in the moment, as if soaking in that calm and strength and allowing it pause to truly take hold.

Greta pressed her lips in a firm smile. She considered something a long while, then went ahead and uttered the words: "I wonder if these things that you're dealing with right now reach back in time and reach forward in time… They seem to, they seem to be things that are touching relationships and maybe perceptions from your past as well as your family's past… and to Molly and the future."

Bee had opened her eyes. Her soft expression confirmed that she was able to take in what Greta was saying.

"When you read a letter, when you write a letter… when you consider the implications… I think your relationship with your mother shifts. I think it might span further back than that, like maybe this antique locket proves. And I think it affects you and Molly too, and Molly's future. You really can be proud of your part in this, Abbey. I don't pretend to understand it all either, but I have a sense that it's honestly making a difference."

Abbey shed tears again, though tonight it was not in solitude. And she reached out warmly to embrace her friend.

The trip to Manhattan in early August was to be an easy one. In preparation for the holiday issue, the senior editor was to be dazzled by various designers and merchandisers with their upcoming lines; Abbey was in for four days of finding herself wined, dined, pampered and -at the hope of many- suitably impressed.

She took the train in Wednesday morning to make a 1:30 meeting in the Fashion District, near Bryant Park. Abbey hadn't bothered to grab lunch; she knew delectable hors d'ouevres would be served during the presentation and throughout the afternoon to complement the fashion walk that would be staged at four o'clock. It was a treat for her to mingle with other editors and a few mid-level buyers, many of them peers in the industry whom she had known for several years. Bee was not in a position to lead any meetings or oversee the afternoon's schedule, and she relished the relaxation. At one point, her mind wandering, she imagined a chance meeting with the freelancer Ben Cole. She was taking her time choosing an assortment from the vegetable platter, but thoughts of the writer proved fleeting as someone else stepped alongside and prodded conversation.

"The new accessories are really my focus," she offered, referring to the upcoming show. "Innovative gift ideas, you know. Lots of interest with the organics and greens of course. And functional, but that's not new."

She and the other woman bantered a little, then chatted about dinner options and a few of the shows that were running off-Broadway. Abbey had never been a devout fan, but she was considering a ticket to one of the Shakespeare plays during this trip.

That evening went by quietly. Abbey cuddled in with the fluffed sheets in her hotel room, watched television and dozed. She had brought a bundle of the letters along, but tonight left them tucked in the lavender ribbon in her suitcase.

Time alone in Manhattan was rejuvenating. Bee had visited but a few times since she had decided to move with Molly, yet the city still held a fascination for her. There was so much life here: everywhere the businesswoman turned, she was caught up in images of motion, dialogue, passion. New Yorkers were committed people, she had long thought -committed to their way of life, to their city, to their community, to their dreams. It could be overwhelming, but also utterly invigorating. Today it reminded Abbey Taft of all the opportunity that awaited her.

The next morning was relaxed, but full: an in-depth discussion around a conference table throughout the early hours, then a lighter meet-and-greet with an array of new designers and blossoming artists. After lunch Bee had the remainder of the afternoon to herself, before a dinner meeting her assistant had managed to schedule with an upper-level manager for one of the boutique retailers. For now, she was on her own, and found herself drawn to the subway for a jaunt down to Battery Park. The street vendors were in abundance; during her stroll Abbey took time to browse. A few pieces struck her and as she bought them she took down information from the merchants and craftsmen. These were organic indeed -some industrial and gritty- charged with simple innovation and a wholesome flair. She couldn't be sure, but at the moment it seemed fitting that these strands of jewelry, the scarf and the trinkets would prove ideal to spotlight in the magazine. *"Editor's Picks,"* she muttered to herself, raising the handmade scarf to her nose for its softness and heavy scent of patchouli. Something about the unassuming appeal of this collection seemed far more authentic and vital. Time, she thought, would tell. But again, she let thoughts wander and enjoyed envisioning the photo shoot: props of natural wood, burlap, or perhaps a subway sign and a chunk of macadam as display for the earrings and metal pendant.

The following evening Bee did in fact indulge in an off-Broadway production of Hamlet. Certainly, she'd seen the play numerous times; nonetheless, Shakespeare was Shakespeare. The soliloquy was extremely well done and moved her nearly to tears. The man seated next to her noticed and, discreetly, offered up his handkerchief. His smile too was kind. After the play when he asked Bee out for a drink, she happily accepted.

The pub a few doors down was quite noisy, prompting the couple to wander further along to a small vintage hotel wherein they found a cozy in-house bar. Abbey ordered a simple taste of white wine; as she held to the stem of the glass, sipping midst the even tempo of conversation, she realized just how well-balanced she was feeling. She was rested and calm... and deliberate.... The thought brought a subtle curve to her lips. So subtle in fact that Ethan, seated across from her, didn't even seem to notice. It was another of her private moments -so new, yet becoming less unfamiliar.

Ethan dipped his grey-eyed gaze and ran the back edge of his hand along Abbey's forearm. It was slow and light and somehow very sexy. Her smile widened. As if on cue, the man ordered her another glass of wine.

It was obvious they had several things in common, and Ethan made her laugh quite a bit which was truly relaxing. But when he pressed close and asked if he might see her to her hotel, Abbey paused just briefly before answering him decisively: "You're adorable, Ethan," she said, "and I find you very attractive but- no. Thank you, no."

He stood politely as she rose to go, and Bee made her way back out into the city noises and streetlights.

As she took the train back home on Saturday, it struck the woman that she had considered several times either emailing or calling Molly's father while she was in the city, to see if he might be available for lunch or coffee, even dinner. But she'd never made it happen, and she wasn't quite sure why not. She and Brian had been good friends, they'd parted amicably, but seeing him could still seem rather complex. That it had occurred to her to reach out was worth noting, she thought. -Inklings about him didn't often cross her mind.

The train shuddered, then sped fluidly once again on its way through the passage from the densely urban outskirts of New York to the more rural heart of New Jersey. Bee watched the apartment buildings zip by, and the warehouse districts… then the broader lines of trees that hid signs of sprawling pharmaceutical complexes or strip malls. Suddenly, staring at length out the window, she came to realize that the shifting light of morning was beginning to show early signs of autumn.

The letters had accompanied her on the trip, but once in Manhattan Bee had decided to give herself a little distance from them after all. Now, into another work week and back to her routine, Abbey pulled the lavender ribbon clear and chose an envelope. The one that struck her first was a note she hadn't often read through:

Abbey Taft,

Your presence is requested

at the 50th anniversary

of Donna & Frederick Lancaster.

Please provide the courtesy of

a reply by June 6, 1995.

Abbey wondered why such an impersonal invitation like this one had found its way midst the other letters. Its tone, too, was a little bewildering: her Aunt Dee and Uncle Frederick were favorites in the family -always lighthearted and spontaneous, generous and caring. Bee could recall another note they had sent to her, back when she'd broken up with a long-term boyfriend in her late twenties. Her aunt had offered very tender insights and words of empathy, seeing to the heart of the situation and communicating it so openly in a way that Abbey's own parents at the time were unable to do.

The memory of it evoked sweetness and nostalgia, a little sadness too in that both her aunt and uncle now were gone. But that precious note was not here. Instead, the strange little invitation.

Taking a longer moment, Bee realized she didn't remember past mention of this party, nor the 50th milestone. In 1995 she herself was building her career -a little careless, perhaps... a little self-involved. If this had reached her by mail sometime back then, she certainly didn't remember it. Maybe that was the point.

Was she meant to feel regret? -A loss of a family connection she might better have sown? Her parents, it was true, were not exceptional at maintaining ties; obviously it applied to Abbey as well. Yet there was no room for blame, when all it came down to now was the fact that Dee and Frederick were gone, and Abbey hadn't made it a priority to dance with them at their anniversary party.

-They wouldn't have thought any less of her, that was sure: they hadn't seen things that way. It was only Abbey who was left struck by the loss. When she penned a reply to this one, the words she wrote were simple:

> Aunt Dee & Uncle Frederick,
>
> I really miss you.
>
> Thank you for being a wonderful
>
> part of my family.
>
> Love from, Bee

As she tucked the letters away for the night, she reached for the little circle of gold, and held it tightly. Closing her eyes, she gauged the weight of it and imagined its beginnings and the message it too might offer. There was stillness and calm... and nostalgia here too. But then came a twitter of discontentment, a flare of skepticism. Abbey opened her eyes and looked closely at the locket, peering hard to make out every mark and scratch. But there was nothing more to it, not tonight. Though suddenly she had the clear realization that it was time to visit Catherine once again.

Chapter Thirteen

"So you know I have to give you a hard time about it," grinned Greta, a wide gesture as she opened the door and crossed the driveway with Bee to the car.

"Well, watch it," returned Abbey. "Keep in mind I could have left you at home." She poked teasingly at her friend's arm and they began the drive together across town.

Again, Catherine's den was a warm haven -oranges and ambers in the front room… a subtle hint of sparkling light that seemed a metaphor for the scope of what went on here. Just a moment after they entered, Catherine bustled through the beaded doorway and welcomed them back into her home. "Sit, sit," she smiled. "And more tea awaits…"

As they gathered at the table, she took a long deliberate look across the room. "Ahh, Abbey, you look well." She nodded in kind emphasis. "And you do too, my friend," she added, reaching to tap a beat Greta's way. "Now Ladies, what brings you here this cloudy afternoon?"

"Well," Bee began slowly, "it's been almost a year since we visited last time… Some amazing things have happened, some amazing things have been uncovered. You were very insightful, Catherine, and I thank you for that. It seems you set some things in motion and I -well- it's been scary, honestly but I've grown through it and continue to grow. Again, I thank you for that. -I think," she snickered. And she added, "But I do think it's time to ask for a little more information."

There was a pause as Catherine let the flow of words settle, silently echo a bit wall to wall. Then she cleared her throat.

"First of all, Abbey, I too thank you but truth be told I set nothing in motion. I am more of a witness than anything else. In our day, witnesses are under-estimated and under-valued but… you are now privy to just how powerful that can be." Again she paused. The words filtered down. "If there is one secret here, in my rooms, and one great hope that may be passed along, it is what you have noticed: it takes no special skill on my part to be a witness in moments that matter, and I invite you to take that jewel from this place and make it your own. More consciously, is what I mean of course. That's all there is to it."

Bee understood. "Greta does that for me all the time," she offered, smiling again. It was pleasant to feel so relaxed, and at long last like she belonged here. Abbey took a full sip of tea.

Catherine jostled her own cup a little noisily. "Well," she said, "you have questions."

Bee explained about the letters and then how more recently the locket had appeared. She kept details short, assuming Catherine could link things together with little pause. Nonetheless as she finished her story and slid the piece of jewelry across the table, Catherine dipped her chin with a certain unfamiliar gravity.

"Extraordinary," she uttered, nearly a whisper.

With care, she took the locket in both hands, thumbing the intricate etchwork, gingerly running her finger round the smooth curve of gold. "It looks fragile," she commented, "but this locket is crafted with great strength and resilience. It will last for centuries," she guessed plainly.

Abbey raised a brow, eager to hear what the psychic would say when realizing no pictures were inside. A delicate give, and the circle opened. Catherine ran her finger there as well, across each face, but she was not surprised at the emptiness therein.

"You are curious," she put to Abbey, lifting her gaze. "A little disappointed, maybe, that there are no images inside?"

Bee nodded, just as Catherine continued: "Hmm... No, not disappointed... Restless... Disturbed. Something about this disturbs you."

"Well I don't know what it's for," Abbey stated quickly. "I didn't know what the letters were for either and that bothered me. I didn't have any idea how they came to me or how the whole post office thing worked itself into being: it made me completely crazy for awhile. But they had some obviousness to them -the words explained themselves. This... this obviously is for me too because it's got the 'B'... but I don't know if it's a gift or a beacon or a reward or a reminder or just something that was lost along the way..."

"It makes her a little uneasy too," piped Greta, "that the whole dynamic at the post office has gone to a new level."

Catherine understood. "Yes. Life goes to new levels, doesn't it?" she articulated, with calm.

Bee was struck by it, and more than a little annoyed; she had the urge to glance up to the corner of the Victorian wallpaper again, but did not. Just as Catherine was about to say something else, Bee asked, "Do you have an organ here?"

"An organ?"

"Oh it just came to mind, honestly... I sort-of could imagine organ music suddenly."

"Well, she is getting the hang of this, isn't she?" the psychic commented back to Greta, who now too was poised in a more assertive lean over the table.

Letting her playful expression subside, Catherine pressed attention even more fully to the little circle of gold in her palm. The tarnished necklace chain, like water, cascaded between fingertips. All three were brought to stare at it a moment, wondering at the inherent textures and the way the light played over the thin metal.

"I have a question now for you," came Catherine's voice, somewhat abruptly. "Abbey Elana, if you were to put pictures herein -who would they be?"

"Obviously Molly, probably on both sides," was the quick response. After a short pause, she commented further, "I could put one of Mom in there. That would be fitting, especially lately... We've been -I've been- working on the relationship... And maybe it would change in a few years? A new love? A stepchild?" she was wondering aloud.

"You know, you're right," replied Catherine, "the pictures you'd put in here may very well change over time." She carefully rubbed a nail on the inside faces. "And you can put photos on either side, Abbey," she went on to say, "but it appears this locket was made to really frame just one. Here- on the right side. You see?"

And she turned the piece, handing it to the younger woman. True, the right had a small inset, encircling. But not on the left.

"As for finding yourself agitated about the outcome or the reasons," she went on, "I suggest resting easy in that for awhile. For a long time, maybe. Hold this gift, accept it, enjoy. Things are mysterious sometimes, thank goodness, and seemingly inexplicable." She lightened. "If your daughter came into this room right now and asked me how the thermostat works and the heat comes up, I couldn't explain that to her. I couldn't even say how the lights come on, not really. But…" and she grinned with obviousness, "I enjoy reading my books by the lamplight, warm here inside despite the changing seasons…" And she paused again, a long moment. "Last time you were here, Abbey, we spoke about Truelove. I think you may have rolled your eyes at its mention… Faith is also an appropriate term. Remember, faith has lots of connotations; lots of facets. I know you're not a religious person and religion holds no exclusivity to this word. So don't let yourself get hung up on that. Faith. It's like an old bell, ringing in the distance -over and over- hearkening you to what comes next. Faith is an enthusiastic affirmation that all is well, despite the confusion and perplexity. Faith is the unending 'yes' -it helps you walk through the fire and also through the grey blurry tunnel, when you're not quite sure. Because there's that bell on the other side, obnoxious sometimes, but still somehow ringing. Reminding you that it's just a tunnel."

She glanced at the locket in Abbey's grasp. "I don't think it will serve us much for me to tell you what notions come to mind about the people who have held the pendant before, or the ones who have worn it…

Because, like I said, there are all kinds of wondrous mysteries in life. You get to choose which ones you want to peek at, which ones you want to leave alone or ignore, which ones you want to return to. There are no requirements here, Abbey, no rules. Not with this locket, not even with your letters. So don't get hung up on that either. Just make of them what you will. That is the invitation, I think. And there is always more to be uncovered underneath, if you want to.

"This locket is for you, that's the gift."

After that, the conversation changed; the women refreshed their tea and chatted more about Molly, about Greta's music, about the day-to-day. Like old friends, they talked, they shared laughter, they wondered aloud. Looking back later, Abbey recalled the visit filled with colors: soaring, blended, rather plain. It was a full and nourishing afternoon.

Chapter Fourteen

'Your future needs you.'

Those were the words that came through in the dream. They were sewn on to the flag that her father was holding, as he stood there in the fog, water up to his knees and rising.

He was smiling to her with his sincere eyes and a firm jaw, hand outstretched. Then he motioned and pointed off into the distance, like a ghost would do, she thought. But somehow it didn't distract her.

That was the way she was to go, he was telling her. That was the way…

And the flag whipped in the wind and the words were in motion and, so moving, that much more alive. *'Your future needs you,'* they read, emphatic even in the dream-silence, even in the rolling grey haze. 'You are needed,' she felt through to her heart.

And as she woke, in a tangle of sheets, Abbey Taft found herself sobbing.

On the way to a dinner date with John Jaffers, Abbey stopped off briefly to visit her mother. Bonaday's was decorated in autumn colors, there were wreaths of fall leaves hanging about the community area and on the front door. Abbey found it hard to believe her birthday was approaching again; she commented about it to Caroline that afternoon. Her mother didn't respond; she was particularly quiet today. Nonetheless, Bee sat with her as the woman nibbled at her early supper.

"Mom," Abbey continued, breaking the silence, "you know, Molly still wants a puppy. I'm thinking of going ahead and getting one for her. I wonder if they let puppies come by here for a visit?... Would you like that?"

This brought Caroline to raise her head; Bee had known it would. In earlier years, her mother always had opinions about pets living inside the house. As she aged, however, the woman had gotten a cat and then another: the pair had been her dear company as the years went by. Abbey knew she missed them, here at the nursing home.

"Well," Bee said, "when we do get a puppy, I'll look into it. If nothing else, when you stay at the house again, Mom, you can play with him. Maybe hold him on your lap."

-That brought her mother to a smile. After a while, the younger woman continued, "I'm going out to dinner tonight with John. I'll tell him 'hi' for you. He always asks about you… But before I go, I wanted to tell you something, Mom." And she cleared her throat, thinking it through.

"I had a dream last night. About Dad. I've been thinking about him a lot lately. I was mad at him for awhile you know because he left us too soon… I've been mad at you too -you left me, in your own way, here, like this… You know…"

Caroline's fork did not hesitate; another bite of meatloaf.

"Well I'm not really angry anymore, Mom. I thought you should know. A part of me is sorry about being angry, part of me isn't, honestly… But a part of me is. Mostly I'm sort-of sad because the reasons I was angry pointed to things that were missing between you and me and Dad… and that makes me sad now. A little bit. But I understand it all better, I think. Mostly, I guess, what I'm trying to say is that I realize now that there were many ways Dad wasn't there for me and there were many ways he wasn't there for you either. And he should have been. We needed him then, we need him now. I-I'm just sorry, Mom, for some of that. And it's not really about being sorry so much as it's just about me letting you know that I think I understand it better. And it felt like I should tell you."

Suddenly Abbey didn't think she could handle her mother's ongoing silence and lack of responsiveness. And she didn't want to spoil the moment. So quickly, she added, "I hope it's all okay, Mom. I-I love you."

And she kissed her mother's cheek, then made way quickly to the door. There was no time for her to see that, in fact, a tear crossed down along her mother's countenance, after all.

Bee didn't really want the evening to get terribly heavy; nonetheless, she found herself apologizing too to John Jaffers. The friend that he was, he simply embraced her and was ready to move on to new conversation. They updated each other about work and the families, but before long Bee turned the dialogue back around. It felt like a knot, slowly releasing hold -easing- when she explained to John about the letters and the locket, and the details in between. John understood perhaps in a way that even Greta could not, because he knew Abbey so very well.

His eyes sparked with realization as she outlined the experience; he gave her two more close hugs before their entrées arrived. As she first tasted the mango salsa on her portion of fish, Bee was already wondering just why she had waited so long to share it all with him.

"You know," she said out loud, "I have some good friends in my life."

And the man agreed with her, beaming. "Yeah, you're a lucky damn work-a-holic," he said. "Now listen, I'm glad you've discovered there's more to life, Bee. And there's even more, after this. So don't forget to keep enjoying yourself, through things like this. You've been much too serious lately, my Dear."

She giggled with him, her face like a little girl's. "As much as I'd like to pore over all the letters with you and demand to know each and every syllable... maybe it's better if we talk about your trip to New York or -something else." John stumbled. "Did you call Brian, huh?" And he baited her well.

Their conversation throughout the remainder of dinner was light, silly, uplifting. As the plates were cleared, he announced that Bee and Molly would join him and Susan the following Friday for a trip to the bowling alley. "And tonight, goddammit, you're having dessert," he added with a sure wink. "And that's that."

Chapter Fifteen

When she opened the post office box this time and found it quite full, Bee laughed outright. She had hoped for this ripe sense of connection; for this fresh anticipation of the discoveries yet to come. And she laughed some more, flashing suddenly to the realization that this emotional torrent had been much like a stereotypical midlife crisis… and finally, *finally*, she was through it far enough to begin feeling once again that life still held new joys and opportunities for her.

-Was that all this was? she wondered, but then she decided it didn't much matter. The exploration mattered, the end result would matter… what she chose to call it would be of little consequence.

Today Abbey indulged in a trip to the Main Street Coffeeshop there in Whelton, and she eagerly tugged open the first new letter. The scrawl on the envelope was child-like; as she unfolded the note inside Bee immediately understood. She couldn't help but hold her breath as she read each word: this letter was from Molly.

'Hi Mama,' it read, the letters imperfect yet precious.

I luv you.

I am glad yu let me

hold yur hand all th days.

-(heart) Molly

Abbey grazed her finger over the paper, soaking in the tenderness of those two sentences. After a moment, she began to study the words instead, and began to wonder if the little girl felt overly pressured to take care of her mother in some way… if there was some clue of role-reversal outlined herein. But the thought was brief. Bee smiled softly and decided such was not the case. This was simply a beautiful little note, from a beautiful little girl. And it served to remind Abbey of a dream she had recently: that even for a child like Molly it was important for her to know she was needed, to know that her place in the family was vital and valued.

When Abbey Taft went home that afternoon she tugged Molly into a close embrace and whispered in her ear: "You're my princess, Sweetheart. And you know what else? You're also my hero."

And, Molly beaming, the two drove out to the animal shelter to find their Aspen.

———————————

At work the next day, things moved along rather smoothly. Bee found herself smiling more than usual, and she considered a lunch date with Janine, but schedules proved a little out-of-sync. At about two o'clock, however, when Ben Cole stopped by to drop off a few research materials along with a completed article, Abbey was happy for the excuse to take a break and enjoy new conversation.

The two wandered to the building lobby, and ordered coffee.

"Exciting news," she proclaimed, and shared details about the grey and white terrier mix who was now adding to Greta's duties back at home.

"I bet Molly can't wait to get home from school today," Ben smiled knowingly.

Abbey agreed. "She's really such a good kid. I'm lucky. I'd like for you to meet her one day."

Ben nodded. -A little less than enthusiastic, Bee thought, but perhaps understandable given her past rapport with him. Today however, something of those dark brown eyes seemed more compelling than usual... and Bee herself was feeling buoyant; she was sure it showed through.

 And just as she smiled directly at him, an image of the engraving on the locket jetted before her eyes. 'B' for Benjamin Cole? Suddenly she wondered. -Could the sign be that obvious?

The writer seated across the table began reciting a few highlights of the article he'd submitted. Abbey didn't even bother trying to listen; she was staring at the movement of his lips, hardly pondering anything except who this man was and what he could mean to her.

The room seemed to widen and become brighter. Her heart jittered, just a little, and she waited for a pause.

"Yeah, thank- thank you, Ben. For getting the article to me early. Listen," and she remembered to smile again, more familiarly this time. "Listen, I would like to ask you something else. Not work-related. Would you like to go to dinner sometime? Off the clock?"

Ben finished his sip of coffee slowly, then took a moment to fidget with the cup as he set it back on the table. "I would like that, Abbey, but-" And he added quickly, catching her gaze with a new focus, "But I'm seeing someone. Right now. And..." He cleared his throat.

While Abbey was more than a little disappointed, his stuttering eased the exchange. She kept watching him, nodding a little as he continued.

"Well, I'm sure it's been noticeable that I've been attracted to you... so now, having dinner sometime would just not really seem appropriate. But- thank you for the invitation."

And his confidence returned as he cocked an eyebrow and held her stare. Bee nodded. She decided not to go any further with the subject *(...I hope this doesn't affect our professional relationship... Oh, well tell me about her – where did you two lovebirds meet?...)* Instead she too gulped at her coffee and allowed the obvious pause, in all its awkwardness. And then she found herself unable to contain another grin, even broader this time.

Ben commented at once, "You look genuinely happy, Abbey," he told her. "More than I've seen you in a long time. Good for you."

She agreed, with a chuckle. And they headed back to the office.

———————————

The following weekend was Bee's 43rd birthday. On Sunday, there was to be a little party, and Abbey had taken a few days off work, but for now she sat between her mother and her daughter on the living room couch and fingered through family photo albums.

"Look at that one, Mommy!" the little girl squealed, pointing at an image of Bee at fifteen, hair curled with a fresh perm. "Gramma, did you see that?!"

Caroline pursed her lips in a tight, lopsided curve. Abbey wasn't sure if she was connecting herself at all with the photographs; but as always she responded easily to Molly's exuberance. With the flames crackling in the fireplace, it was a warm and cozy interaction. Bee felt right where she was supposed to be; it was truly revitalizing.

"Now Girls," she said suddenly, "I think our sleepover won't be complete unless we have popcorn. Mom? Does that sound good?"

Caroline nodded. "With hot apple cider," she replied dryly.

Bee overlooked the tone. "Hmm," she thought aloud. "I can wing it. Good idea, Mom."

Molly cheered, then pointed at another photo. "Gramma," she asked, "who is that next to you?"

Bee watched for awhile, but the older woman didn't respond. To Molly, it didn't seem to matter much; the little girl came up with her own answer. "Oh, it must be your friend from next door, Gramma. Ooh, look at this one -it's a doggie like Aspen! I didn't know you had a doggie, Gramma!"

Bee had ventured into the kitchen, but couldn't help but hear her mother's firm and definitive answer this time: "No, no dogs," she said emphatically. "Cats. Milo and Adelaide. But they were at my blue house on Cascade Street."

Abbey smiled. The memories they all shared now were criss-crossed and interspersed, often broken and incomplete. But it didn't have to be sad, at least not always. Life was mysterious, she acknowledged, thinking back to the words Catherine had said. Strange and confusing, unpredictable and sometimes heartbreaking. But always mysterious.

"Popcorn, Girls!" she called, re-entering the living room as Molly tried to engage her grandmother in playing fetch with the puppy. The room was noisy and busy.

"Hey Girls," Abbey observed, loud and bright. "This is just how a home should be on a Friday night. Thanks for being my family."

The next morning Bee drove her mother, Molly and Aspen south near Philadelphia, where her sister Kate lived. Molly was thrilled to show the puppy to her cousins -she and the boys chased the little terrier round and round the yard for over half an hour.

After the greetings, Caroline immediately made her way inside and demanded a hot cup of tea. Kate raised a brow at the tone but seemed impressed when Abbey reassured their mother and quickly brewed a pot.

"So how are you, Abbey?" her sister asked, tidying the morning dishes before she sat down at the table.

"Oh I'm really well," Bee told her. "Work is work, but it hasn't been too crazy lately. I had a nice few days in Manhattan recently -really enjoyed it."

"Did you see Brian?"

"No. It crossed my mind but... I just didn't feel like it while I was there, so I didn't force it."

"That man could reach out to you more often," Kate said. "Well, at least to Molly. Does he call?"

"On her birthday and Christmas. Not much." But she smiled. "Honestly I'm glad about it. I don't want to share custody -so this is easier."

Kate's husband Jeff wandered in. "Bee's always been able to take care of herself," he gibed, kissing his sister-in-law and then Caroline.

"It's Molly I was concerned about," Kate said. "But yes, I'm sure they're both fine."

"Brian does send checks," mentioned Abbey, then she grinned with obviousness across the table. "Not all of us managed such a fine catch..."

Jeff chuckled playfully. "Well look, Ladies, I promised the guys a game of putt-putt. Thought I'd take them along with Molly; get us all out of your way so you can catch up."

"Aww, see he is a great catch."

Kate reached up for a kiss, and patted him as he went on his way. "Yeah, I'm lucky," she agreed. "He's a good guy."

Abbey poured the tea, and took a seat as well. Caroline gulped rather quickly, despite the fresh heat of the liquid. "Where is John-Wyatt?"

she suddenly asked, looking up from her cup and surveying the room.

"Oh Mom, he's back at your house. You'll see him soon. Do you miss him?"

"He drinks mid-morning tea with me," she said, and began tapping the table a little nervously. "He's never late. I hope he's all right."

"Mom, we're here visiting Kate and Jeff and their family today. They wanted to see you. Kate is drinking mid-morning tea with you instead, and I'm sure John-Wyatt is just fine back at the house. You'll see him in a few days."

That helped the tapping. And for awhile, Kate and Abbey continued their conversation. Then Caroline grew nervous again. Kate asked if she might like to watch television, and took her into the living room. Not long and Kate returned to the kitchen, rejoining her younger sister at the table.

"She doesn't remember much at all, does she?" Kate commented.

Abbey shook her head.

"Well thank you for doing so much for her. I'd like to visit more, but every three or four months is about all I can seem to squeeze in."

"Yeah I know. It's fine. I still talk about you to her, and we look at pictures sometimes."

"You're good with her Abbey. I don't know if I expected that from you... Thank you."

The two shared further details about work and the children. After checking on Caroline, Kate announced she was planning a berry pie for the birthday celebration. With that, she pulled an assortment of bowls and a pie tin from the cupboard. Abbey enjoyed watching as her sister mixed flour and the other dry ingredients, then added just the right amount of water, without peeking at a recipe.

"It's fascinating," she observed, "what a little homemaker you became…"

Kate wasn't overly amused. "I don't think you ever quite pegged me," she said, then added, "Well we probably didn't peg each other too well, come to think of it." And she shifted her stance. Then she faced Abbey and continued, "Are you st- No. Nevermind."

"What?"

"No, it's really not fair of me to ask."

"Oh Kate. Katie… Come on, you can't do that. You don't see me often enough to do that."

Kate managed a lighter expression. Then, with a deep breath, she put to her sister, "You're really good with Mom, like I said. But I was just wondering… Are you still just as angry with her and Dad?"

Abbey was quick to answer the question, glad for it really. Too often, she thought, she and Kate couldn't navigate much depth to their conversations. Without holding back, she said, "No -well- yeah. I mean, I've kind of been looking at another layer of that recently. In my defense though I'm not mad like it seems you think I am, Kate. I mean I'm not 15 anymore, you know?" And she slowed. "I have found some new ways to let that old stuff go." And she smiled, just slightly. "-Maybe that's what a midlife crisis is after all, huh?... You're almost 50, Kate, haven't you scoured your life history, trying to figure out if there's anything else that can be sorted through in order to get yourself on the right trajectory? You know, the one that'll lead to more peace or more fulfillment or more forgiveness or something? At least a fresh perspective."

Kate didn't answer, a silent response. She didn't seem very moved, and went back to kneading the dough. "I grew up a long time ago, Abbey," she finally said, rather flatly. "That's what's always pissed me off about you."

Bee chuckled. "Well see, you've still got some old anger in there... See, Kate?" And she reached to rub gently at her sister's shoulder.

"Yeah," Kate shrugged admittedly. "We've all got old baggage, I guess. It's just never been as simple as being a teenager who's mad at her parents. -Maybe as the first-born, I always wanted to stick up for them... and you wanted to rebel. Maybe that was the problem."

"Yeah, good insight... Standard family dynamics, I guess, play a part. Why not? We all have our roles to fill." And Bee paused, watching her sister work a rolling pin over the stretch of dough. After a long moment she added, "But I have not been angry at Mom and Dad all this time, Kate, I want you to know that. I wouldn't have wanted to live my life these past 20 years with that kind of emotion just under the surface. That seems... dangerous." And again, she chuckled a little. "But it's come up this last year or so -maybe with Mom in the nursing home, I don't know...

"You know, I don't sift through this stuff just to dredge up old wounds... I do it to understand better, and right now I do it because it's always seemed like there's some little mystery to be solved. That it'll help me feel better somehow."

Kate faced her again, now having pressed the dough into all the edges of the pie pan. Abbey gauged her stare.

"I am not searching for the ideal childhood, Kate," she explained, somewhat firmly. "I am a grown-up and I get it that life comes with all its ups and downs and inexplicable details... But those little twinges of regret, or past confusion, or past anger or missed opportunities... I don't know, they're like little signposts to me. And what I've realized lately -that emptiness I always thought was between me and Mom, was actually a thing between her and Dad. It probably had nothing to do with me." Again, she lightened. "-Kind of frees me up, which is a really good thing."

"Yes," Kate offered, "it's good to let yourself off the hook." And she turned to mix the strawberries, raspberries, blackberries and sugar. With a forced grin, she pulled a bag of chocolate chips from the refrigerator and tossed a small handful into the bowl.

Abbey refused to change the subject. "Katie, you're still trying to defend them." And she pointed playfully at her sister. "It's okay for me to have a relationship with them that's different than yours."

She half-expected her sister to get very upset, but Kate didn't. It was refreshing, and brought Abbey's gaze to soften entirely. "You'd be proud of me -I told Mom recently that I wasn't angry anymore and that I'd reached a new understanding. I don't know, these days, if that gets through to her consciously but... it seemed important to say it; to take advantage of the opportunity to say it."

Finally Kate's expression eased too. She invited Abbey's help weaving together the top lattice of the pie crust. But she didn't say anything.

After brushing the flour from her hands, Abbey dug into her purse and retrieved a little cloth satchel. As Kate turned from the oven, Bee offered it to her. "Have you seen this before?" she asked.

Kate opened the small colored bag, and the golden locket spilled out into her hand. She didn't treat it with particular fragility; Abbey was sure she knew her sister's answer.

But then, as Kate handed the necklace back, she faced Bee and told her, "It looks just like the one Mom has. Only -you know- Mom's letter has the different style."

"What?" Abbey was incredulous. Her tone was completely incongruous to the casual way Kate had explained. And now, her sister had turned again back to the kitchen counter, pulling rice and a can of chicken stock out of the pantry. She began chopping carrots and onions.

"Kate?"

"Oh, the 'B' on Mom's locket is in a different font, I guess you'd say. I don't know -it was engraved a long time ago. Do you call that a font?"

"Katie, I haven't seen this locket before, I didn't know Mom had one. What are we talking about?"

"Go into Mom's jewelry box sometime, Abbey. You'll find hers... If you got this other one out of storage or the old trunk or something, well, it was probably for her sister." She happened to glance over at Bee, and saw at once the continued puzzlement. Inside, Abbey's heart was racing.

Kate offered more. "Gran had these made, just before the twins were born. She was so excited, she used to say, to be having twins back in the day." A smile crossed her face, with fond memories of her grandmother.

"...Twins?" Abbey rose to the counter. "Twins?"

"What is wrong with you? You know, Mom's sister, Aunt Hannah."

"Mom was a twin?"

"Of course she was a twin, Abbey." Bee's expression held, obviously still baffled. "Don't you remember? I mean, we talked about this, well, at least a few times with Gran, over the years. Mom, you know Mom, she doesn't like to talk about sad things very much."

"Wait. So. 'Hannah' doesn't begin with a 'B'…"

Kate rolled her eyes. "Neither does 'Caroline'… Gran had these made before the girls were born. The letter is for 'Baby.' I don't know, maybe it was the thing to do back then to make lockets for babies…"

There was a long moment of silence. All Abbey could manage, finally, was, "Wow."

Emptiness, Sadness, Anger, Something-missing… It was all right here before her, right here in the palm of her hand: *Grief.* It had taken form, in so many ways, over the decades. It had been handed down, and passed over, and shoved aside, until people didn't even know what to call it anymore. Clarity, along with endless new questions, cascaded down through Abbey's thoughts in a torrent.

"Did Mom ever talk about Aunt Hannah? How did she die? How old were they when it happened? …My gosh, that is so awful…"

"I don't remember Mom saying much. Babies sometimes died back then, more easily, as terrible as that is… Hannah was about one, I think. It was like SIDS -she just died in her sleep."

Abbey whimpered, "Oh God. Mom was probably in the crib with her… And, being one, and having a twin sister and then she's suddenly gone forever… God, you'd feel like a part of you was just amputated."

Kate agreed.

"Guilt, grief, everything..." Abbey continued, pulling from her ongoing thoughts. "And how do you sort all that when you're a baby? Shit." And she faced her sister. After a time, there were tears in her eyes. "Kate, I found this locket, and I thought it was for me. The 'B,' it just... it just seemed like it was for me... How could I be so self-involved?"

With a kind gaze, Kate replied, "No, it's never been all about you, Abbey." And she reached, to touch away her sister's tears. "Then again, it has always been about you. Families are like that, you know. They're like weird lenses -one view super imposed over another- where you see all generations forever back in time, and all the interconnections... And then you can also see, like a microscopic view, right back down to yourself and your own handprint; your own single narrow perspective.

"It's a mind-fuck," she added, trying to make Abbey laugh. "But that's the way things are." She smiled, "All those 'inexplicable details...'"

At once Abbey stepped around the counter and embraced her sister. Like never before.

After that, she went to the living room and hugged her mother, then urged the woman to the piano bench. "Let's play the old duets, Mom. C'mon, I need you." -It seemed, for her mother's sake, the simplest and yet the most meaningful thing she could say. At least for now.

Later, after dinner and with Kate's help, Abbey showed the locket to her mother. "So pretty," Caroline said, beaming at the trinket. But she did not recognize its significance. Again, they turned through the pages of old photo albums, but could not find a picture of Little Hannah.

Kate spoke up, "I know I've seen one of her," she said. "Probably with Gran and Grandpa's old things. I'll have to go up in the attic. When I find it, I'll make a copy and send it to you, Abbey."

Bee thanked her, then turned to Molly. "A couple of rounds of 'Go-Fish,' Sweetie, then it's time for us to drive home."

Molly cheered, and hurried off to gather her cousins for the play. Then she turned back, returning to smack a noisy kiss at her mother's cheek. "Happy Birthday, Mommy!" she giggled. "Don't tell anyone, but I'll let you win one time." And she bounded off, calling her cousins' names.

It was warm enough on Sunday for a game of croquet. Everyone was eager to play, in celebrating Abbey's birthday. Molly helped show young Garrett how to hold the mallet, and John strategically set up the wickets, offering a wink to his wife as he brought her the dark green ball. "Defeat is in your future, Dr. Jaffers," he teased, kissing her cheek. Even Caroline joined in, chuckling a little midst the activity.

For lunch, they gathered inside, ordered pizzas and drank iced tea. Molly and Garrett played rather quietly while the adults chatted. Greta, ever insightful, could tell Abbey wanted to keep it light; nonetheless, before cutting the cake she stood up and asked for everyone's attention.

"We're all proud of Bee, and happy to celebrate her big day," Greta began. "And I know we all want cake, but before we get going, I thought we should go around the circle and each say a few words. Something special about Abbey, or some wishes for her new year ahead, or a fun memory you have of her. Whatever strikes you." She glanced around the room, then added, "I'll start. …Last year, I took Abbey to dinner for her 42nd birthday, and a friend joined us. The three of us talked about a lot of things -the past, the future, the possibilities ahead. Bee," she grinned, a little mischievously, "was a bit uneasy… somewhat resistant. I think a part of you," she continued, facing her friend, "was worried that life was winding down. But you let the ideas we all talked about percolate and, well, you've really turned your resistance around. I think we can all see this year that you're looking ahead. More openly for what's on the horizon. To me, that's a great gift to yourself. And I'm really proud of you, Bee. Happy Birthday."

John piped up next. "There's no formula for life. As a kid, a young adult, through the chapters of adulthood…" He grinned broadly across the table. "I've known Abbey Elana and Mrs. Taft -Caroline- for ages. And I have to say that I admire these girls for their attitude and persistence, gutsiness and sense of humor… You two, well, you face life." And he set his arm around Caroline's shoulder. "Bee, in the past I've seen you delight in all that life has to offer," and he brightened playfully, "over-indulging at times… I've seen you wrestle and combat with life, I've seen you disappointed by it, I've seen you pursue. But mostly, you truly-" and he paused a moment, thoughtful. "-You explore life, Bee, in a conscious way. You're eager to have a full and authentic experience, and I'm really proud of you for it and happy for you, because it's not always easy or comfortable, but it's made you richer and more…" Again, he chose the words deliberately, squeezing Caroline a little closer. "It's made you richer in so many ways, and more compassionate, and maybe more yourself somehow. I love you so very much. Happy Birthday."

With that, he stood and gave Abbey a warm hug. Bee kissed his cheek. "Well thank you John," she exclaimed, nodding too to Greta. "What a sweet gift you're giving me…"

Everyone smiled, though Greta noticed Caroline and the children eagerly eyeing the yellow and white swirls of frosting. "I'll pass around birthday cake," she said. "But Janine, don't let me interfere."

Taking the cue, Janine gazed across at Abbey. "I haven't known you very long," she said. "But I can relate to what everyone's saying. Even though we don't spend a lot of time together, you're a very good friend. I'm sure it's because of just how you do interpret life, the way you do choose to experience things… I also really admire your wisdom and your candidness, and how strong a woman you are, professionally and otherwise. You've become a role model for me, and I thank you. If I were to make a wish for you in your 43rd year, I guess I would hope that things keep getting better and better for you, maybe with a little unexpected amazement and joy added in too. Happy Birthday, Abbey."

Molly went on to say just how thankful she was for her mother, during this important day especially, because the yellow flowers on the cake were her favorite. Susan added that her birthday wishes for Bee included better luck at the bowling alley, and maybe a new romance. "I don't worry over it, after all these years," she gibed. "But let's be honest… Abbey, you're a better friend to my husband than I am. Obviously I'd love for your new year to include a new someone-special just so I could be a little less jealous!" And she grinned wide. John leaned in to give her a reassuring kiss.

Everyone laughed except Caroline, who rather gruffly ordered another piece of cake. Molly chimed in too, raising her plate, and Garrett followed along with a hopeful smile. Abbey moved to cut a few extra slices. As she offered more to the others, a soft word came from her mother.

"Strong," Caroline uttered, eyes up to look at her daughter. "You've always been strong," she said. "And successful." With that, she took the second piece of cake and bit into it with little delicateness, her focus now upon her fork and the sweet dessert.

Some of the others glanced to Abbey, meeting her gaze supportively. "Thank you, Caroline," Greta said.

John added, "Yes, I can tell you're proud of Sweet Abbey, like we are," he nodded. "And I can see the cake is scrumptious, right Molly? Let's eat!"

After the party, Greta stayed awhile to help clean up. Abbey thanked her for another very special birthday celebration. And she squinted over at the woman, then wondered aloud, "Are you my Truelove, Greta Duvall? I mean, you take such good care of me (not to mention Molly)... You're so thoughtful and smart and funny and I love how you view the world. You are an amazing person. I do, I love you." And she reached to press her lips to Greta's hand, as they finished tidying the kitchen table.

Greta sat down, sipping at her iced tea. "I'm flattered, Bee. And you're right, we'd make a great couple... but, I do think the love Catherine was referring to last year was all about yourself. You know that, right?"

"Hmm." And Bee sat alongside her. "Guess I hadn't known it, but sure, I suppose that's what this past year has been about. ...Damn, you are so deep, Greta!"

And they chuckled together. After a moment, Abbey continued, "Talking about it does make me realize though that I do actually want a long-term relationship again. Someday. I mean not right now, not this minute but… I'm getting closer."

Greta nodded in agreement. "You have grown a lot, that'll mean your next relationship will be very new, very different from others in your past. Exciting. I am excited for you, Abbey. I meant what I said today: You've come a long way in realizing there's a great future waiting. Another 43 years of wide open opportunity. And that is really exciting."

Smiling to her, Bee blew another kiss her way.

Greta whispered playfully, "I'm not your truelove…"

They quieted a while, and sipped more tea.

"You know," Greta then piped, "your Mom was great today. She meant what she said. 'You're strong, you're successful…' She believes that, Abbey. And it's an obvious lead-in to other things she feels about you too."

"Yeah, I got that," Bee said. It was true that she'd been able to soak in not only the words and intent her mother had shared this afternoon, but also the words unspoken. "What a great weekend…" she added, somewhat lazily, with a stretch and a yawn. "Oh my gosh!" she then exclaimed, turning abruptly. "Greta! I haven't even told you!"

"What?"

"-The locket, my sister Kate, oh my gosh-" And she took a quick breath. "I showed the locket to Kate, asking if maybe she'd seen it before. I don't know why, it just sort-of happened. I don't know. The locket just suddenly seemed like a family heirloom or something."

Greta nodded, her eyes bright as she heard the details unfold.

"Turns out it is... And Kate acted like it was no big deal. She's seen another locket just like this one, in Mom's old things. My Mom *-she has one.* And this one," Bee tugged the necklace from around her neck, on which now hung the little post office key along with the locket. "This one belonged to my aunt, Mom's twin sister. Aunt Hannah. She died as a little baby.

"My God, Greta, I never remembered Mom had a twin. I mean, what's wrong with me that I didn't remember??"

Greta reached to finger the locket again. "Wow," she muttered, in awe. "I don't know, Bee. I guess it makes this a little less of a mystery though somehow, doesn't it?"

"Huh?"

"Well, it's not just a locket out of the blue, signifying you and love and some unknown connection. Now we know this locket is about your aunt and your family and you and love and... well, that sort-of makes more sense to me somehow."

"But why didn't Catherine mention something like this?" A tinge of the anger flared again. "How is it all possible?... And why -why did I forget about Hannah? I'm sure we talked about her back when I was a kid. You know, family tree stuff, photo albums..."

After a pause, Greta said, "Well, sometimes we choose not to remember. Maybe it was too sad for you to take in."

"Maybe I was a self-involved kid." The red in her eyes blurred a little.

Again, she breathed deeply.

"-Your mom had a twin. Wow…"

In hearing her, Abbey's gaze softened a bit. She smiled to her friend. "You're a trooper to go through this with me, Greta."

After another long moment Greta said, "Your mom called you strong and successful. Maybe she meant it, because you're the second daughter who survived."

With a little gasp, Bee went teary again. "Do you think she resents me?"

"Oh no, Abbey. You're her daughter. Maybe she was scared to death -subconsciously- you wouldn't survive. Maybe that made her tougher on you to make you strong. Or maybe that made her keep a distance. Or, who knows?"

"Maybe some part of her resented me. I would understand."

This time, Greta didn't disagree. She set an arm around Abbey's shoulder.

"The death of a baby is impossible for a family, of course," Greta said. "But there are so many tragedies and triumphs that define us. And you know it's not your fault, right? I mean, fault is not the issue. It never is. It's just -it's just something that happened and we have to process this stuff, layer after layer, and support each other through it, being aware, letting go… I don't know. Something like that."

Bee was crying. And Greta held her tighter, and let her cry some more.

Chapter Sixteen

The following week, there was an early morning dream that gently wakened Abbey. She couldn't remember the details, but it had been soft, consuming, somehow tender and reassuring. As she opened her eyes, Bee found herself staring at the curtains, watching the light change when morning came.

It was simply pastel orange sunshine today, sifting through. And the sky was cloudless, with no misted haze to blur the dawn. Abbey breathed it in. Despite being early November, it felt instead like the awakening of a new spring.

It was Saturday, and Molly had a playdate at a friend's house. As she drove home that morning after dropping off her daughter, Bee picked up a deli sandwich and decided to make it a quiet day for herself. With Aspen at her heels, she went upstairs and gathered the bundles of letters, then sat back into a comfortable lean in the recliner.

A few of the letters that she'd read before caught her attention:

> Abbey,
> The day we met,
> my heart skipped a beat.
> I adore you.
>
> > -Unsigned

> B.
> You're so boring.
> You don't care about anything and you're
> not too deep, not too shallow. High school
> is about exploration: You're sidestepping.
> Is it fear? Low esteem? A control trip?
> Arrogance?
> -I don't care anymore.
> Have a great life.
>
> > -S.T.

> *By the way, here's a poem for you-*
> When I was born,
> my eyes were bright and glowing
> with the anticipation of sheer possibility.
> Today my gaze is greyed;

dimmed with time and loss.

I am not a stone, like some of the others,

but I am changed.

And another:

> I wish I could kiss your lips again.
> You are beautiful, Abbey. I know
> we're on the softball team together,
> and the other girls think it's gross,
> but I know it can't be wrong. Not
> when it feels so good to hold you.
>
> -J.N.

Abbey smiled to herself, remembering the awkward embrace she'd shared with Julie Newnan back in 11th grade. Indeed, it had been an electrifying kiss. She let her fingers drift over the handwriting of this letter. Julie Newnan…

The girls never kissed again; Abbey had never allowed herself to be alone with Julie after the moment in the locker room. She hadn't wanted to be gay; as a teenager she didn't think she could handle all the difficulties associated with it. -The shame, the embarrassment, the teasing, the not-fitting-in.

Besides that, Abbey truly had feelings for boys too. Back then, it had been a jumble in her head and, at times, she had found herself torn with a deep desire not to betray the more sensitive friends in her circle. Like

Julie. And so Bee had remained distant altogether, rather than risk confusing Julie with her own swirl of emotions. In college, she'd had more casual -though somewhat more intimate- encounters. It had taken several years for her to feel confident enough in her own feelings to offer much attachment to anyone else.

Now, looking back, Abbey was able to smile. It was one of the gifts of adulthood not to have to define herself by such limiting parameters or perspectives. And she giggled out loud. -Bisexuality was one very small part of all that.

"Whew," she muttered, brushing her hair aside and taking up a pen.

> 'Glad we all made it through
> high school,' she wrote. 'Julie,
> S.T., Unsigned, you all helped
> teach me about myself, about
> love, about not taking the easy
> road just for the sake of it.
> I appreciate your important part
> in my life. I hope each of you
> is happy today.
>
> -Fondly, Abbey'

With that, Bee thumbed through a few more letters. Each one was priceless, indeed, and today she felt no hint of anger or bewilderment… only openness and gratitude.

Then she patted Aspen and rose to wander outside. The fresh air was somewhat warm; Bee retrieved the letters along with her sandwich, and went back out to the porch.

As she watched the puppy scamper about the yard, she pulled free another blank notecard. This one had a flower on the front. Within, she wrote simply:

Dear Aunt Hannah,

I am so sorry about so many things.

God, I hope it wasn't too terrible or scary

or confusing, that year for you... and the

transition to not being here anymore.

Certainly it was terrible and scary and

confusing for your parents and your sister.

It continues today -it's terrible to me and

scary and confusing too... I imagine there's

a reason you were taken so young and

so suddenly, but it's hard to know why.

What I do know is that you've been missed.

I love you, and I thank you for being my family.

-Love from Abbey

As she re-read the note, Bee thought of several things she might add, but put down the pen anyway. She watched Aspen a while longer, then bit into the sandwich. Here she was, 43 years old, writing a letter to a ghost -an angel- who had shared her family name for just a short time nearly 80 years ago. It seemed very strange, but something of it was also just right.

"There's nothing else," she mouthed to Aspen, chewing her lunch, "that I'd rather be doing. Guess I should be cleaning the house but... you know..."

The puppy yipped, having come closer to beg for a taste of the turkey. Abbey grinned at him, and offered a pinch. "You're a cutie," she said. "Molly was right all along, wasn't she? Smart girl we have, Aspen."

Again, he yipped happily. With his help, Bee finished the sandwich. She yawned, sipped at a bottle of water, and eyed the stack of papers. Then, with deliberateness, she lifted the pen once more.

Chapter Seventeen

When the photo arrived in the mail, Abbey's fingers shook a little as she pulled open the envelope to take first glance. Of course it was a reprint of an old, faded black & white -dark, grainy, shadowed. Nonetheless there were her Grandpa and Gran smiling up at her, their arms tucked tight around their sweet-faced baby girls. The adults looked so young, so perfect. Bee imagined all they'd been thinking at that moment when the image had been taken: Pride, joy, a bit of new-parent angst at the recent birth of their firstborn children... They looked like this was just another day at home there in the living room, two tiny girls bundled close to their hearts. They had no idea of the sorrow that awaited, just months into the future. Again, it all made Abbey very sad, a little confused. But she knew there was nothing to remedy it: she simply felt sad, in response to an utterly wrenching moment in time.

Turning the photo in her hand, she saw that Kate had included two copies. Abbey took the cue and, pulling scissors from a drawer, trimmed out the close-up of little Hannah. Unclasping her necklace, she clicked open the locket and inserted the picture.

"As it was always meant to be," she said aloud, and tucked the other image into her purse.

On her way to work, she stopped in at Bonaday's for breakfast with her mother and clasped the locket about Caroline's neck. "This one was Hannah's locket, Mom," she explained, kissing the woman's cheek. "Do you want to talk about her? Do you remember who Hannah was?"

Her mother didn't give any sign she recognized the name.

Bee prodded further, "Do you want to talk about Dad? Now that I'm older, I'd love to have more of the scoop about you and Dad. You know, from an adult perspective, your parents' relationship is always different than you saw it as a kid..."

Caroline kept spooning her oatmeal.

"Well, I love you," Bee added. "Today's music day, have a good time at the sing-a-long. I'll see you again soon."

Driving away, Abbey indulged in wondering how it might have been, all these years, to have had a doting aunt to look to, in trying to better understand her mother. Maybe Hannah would have had an engaging sense of humor, maybe she'd have kindled a girlish giddiness in Caroline -perhaps it was her absence that took such lightheartedness away.

There had been a disconnect between Caroline and Donald Taft. Abbey had seen it all her life, though only in recent years had she truly defined it as a thing to be considered... Was there a gap -a wound- in Caroline's heart that made it impossible for complete intimacy with anyone, ever again, after the loss of her twin? Had Donald been aware, when they were younger... or had it appeared with more obviousness only later in their marriage?

Again, Abbey could imagine the rounded, smiling face of an elderly aunt gazing through to her, as if an integral part of her life all along… as if ready and poised to offer some insightful and sensitive advice. But she faded back and away, voiceless, only leaving Abbey to wonder.

Work that morning included a few easy phone calls, some unexpected and rather tedious editing on a past-due article submission from Sam Beauregard, and a slew of emails to answer. Overall, a light few hours. It occurred to Abbey that in fact her time at the office lately had been rather calm -as she'd been doing at home, she took a conscious moment to breathe in the realization. This was good, she thought to herself, exhaling audibly. This was good.

It had been nearly three months since she and Janine had made a lunch date: Abbey looked forward to their meeting today at the café, and she hoped Janine's morning had been similarly moderate so that they could enjoy a leisurely meal together. Happily, the younger woman entered the restaurant in a breezy motion, eager as well for a relaxing chat. Quickly they compared schedules and decided on a full-course; with a grin Abbey ordered an appetizer and invited the waiter to take his time.

"Ahh," she said, turning back to Janine. "It's great to see you. We should do this at least once a month."

"How about twice?" Janine quipped. "We could plan on every other Tuesday or something."

With a quick nod, Abbey agreed. "So tell me how you are? How's Garrett doing these days?"

"Garrett's actually great."

"Yeah, he's growing up! I noticed at the birthday party."

"He really loves Molly, by the way. She's a good big sister." And Janine grinned at her, taking a sip of the orange-infused water.

"Molly's a great kid, all around. I'm so proud of her." Then she paused, just momentarily. "But tell me how you are, Janine. Any news on the divorce?"

"Yes, it's moving along. Won't be finalized until early next year; it takes awhile. But I'm doing better mentally with it." She spoke brightly. "And Garrett's adjusted fine. He's three nights with me then two with his Dad... Right now he thinks it's fun, like a sleepover."

The spinach dip arrived, each of the women sunk a tortilla.

"Well, if he's handling it so well, then you and Gabe must be too, at least on some level. Garrett's got to pick up on that, right?"

Janine nodded, swallowing. "Mm, yeah. It's not the scenario I planned for my little boy -to have two different homes and two different bedrooms. And a spare 'stepmom' already at three years old... but he'll be fine."

"You look okay too, Mommy."

Again, she nodded. "I've realized it's going to be all right. Really. So yeah, I'm good right now."

Again, they munched at the appetizer. "Any dating?" Abbey prodded.

"Oh well, a little," her friend confessed, nibbling. "But nothing too amazing. Just some casual dinners and a little dancing. Oh, and a movie. Oh, and that odd trip to Philly for some wholesalers' gemstone show…" And she giggled, then between chuckles offered further details.

They laughed together, and as the lunch salads arrived, Janine turned the conversation to ask if Bee had been seeing anyone.

"No, not for awhile. You know, I've been doing my soul-searching this year… I haven't been much interested in dating."

Janine agreed. "I should probably be doing that too, but I guess after the fighting and lousy relationship Gabe and I had those last months together, I was ready for some fun."

"Of course," Bee said, cutting a strip of tempeh in her salad. "Fun is important."

After a pause, Janine asked, "How are things with your Mom? She seemed well at the party, but I know it's got to be hard on you sometimes."

Bee smiled across the table. "Aww, thanks for being so thoughtful," she said. "Yeah, Mom's good too. She's getting a little more finicky, but she's good. Somehow it seems we're communicating a little better. I'm not sure how."

Janine's expression tugged for more.

"I don't know, maybe I'm just bouncing thoughts off her. She's not necessarily responsive but somehow it's making more sense to me. At least some things." And she shrugged. "But there are still lots of issues. Still… it's manageable." She smiled again.

Janine poured a bit more dressing on her salad, then posed a new question. "Abbey," she began, a little slowly. "When you were just starting out-"

"You mean 'young'?" Bee teased.

Janine giggled again. "I mean young-*er*... You know, my age..."

"Um-hmmm..."

"Well, when you were my age, did you have a plan for what your next ten, fifteen years were going to look like? Did any of it -anything- work out like you'd hoped it would?"

Certainly it was a question Abbey too had pondered lately. "I don't know if I have the answer to that," she offered plainly. "And that's kind of depressing, isn't it?"

Janine was uncertain, but she held her smile, waiting in earnest.

Bee cleared her throat, thinking. "Well, let's see... Yes, certain things worked out. Maybe not the specifics. Like I knew for sure I was going to work hard and deliberately and build a career. I didn't map it out, but it's worked out in a way like I thought it might...

"Family was never so important to me, it wasn't my focus. But I did want kids. So, even though the circumstances were unexpected, I guess that worked out too..."

"What about the deeper stuff?" Janine continued. "I mean, do you feel like life is fulfilling? Do you feel like dreams actually came true? Do you have major regrets about anything?" She exhaled audibly, an attempt to lighten the inquiry. "I really don't mean to grill you... I just, well, the disappointment of the divorce is something I am feeling better about but still, it makes me question how much control I actually have about my future and the course my life takes. I just need a little reassurance, I guess," she admitted.

Abbey reached across the table, as she did with Greta sometimes, and clasped her friend's hand. "We all need that," she said, squeezing a little. "I can't guarantee anything at all for you or even for myself," she said. "But the world is generally a happy place, you know. I mean, we can expect happiness. We can anticipate that to be the default. Terrible or unexpected twists and turns may happen -they probably will- and they may change your course but they don't define you. And they don't have to change your ultimate goals or your outlook... You do have a say in all that."

Janine's gaze brightened even more.

"I can't explain how it all works, and that's frustrating sometimes... Because some things do seem to come easy for some people and other things don't, and then there's this setback or that interruption or whatever... But, I don't know..."

Now Janine squeezed back at Abbey's fingers, and patted supportively. Softly, she added to what Bee was saying, "Sometimes we think we have all the answers, then it just falls apart. But, we manage..."

"Yeah..." And Bee held the young woman's stare. "There's something more to it than that, though. There's some thread of constancy, there's some underlying denominator that doesn't change... I'm still trying to figure out what that is. It may be as simple as Love, or Faith, or that default Happiness... I don't know. And it seems kind of glib, when talking about the nights you cry in your pillow because you don't know how you're going to pull yourself out of bed in the morning and manage the day, or how you're going to pay the bills sometimes or send your kid to college, or when there's some really terrible thing that happens. Still, there's something underlying it all, *something…*" And she squeezed back one more time, then let go of Janine's hand. "But I do know that you're going to be fine, that Garrett's fine, that I'm fine. And if we keep striving for that next thing -whatever it is- well, it does get closer. And you do have power over that momentum. And maybe, maybe, the most important thing is not even the end-result or the goal you're shooting for, so much as the way you go about getting there and the attitude you keep while it's all coming together… I think that often defines us more than the accomplishments or the acquisitions or the milestones."

Nodding, Janine thanked her. "I didn't mean to get all heavy," she said.

"Are you kidding? That's why I like our lunches," Bee grinned, bringing them both to laughter once more.

As the waiter came by with the check, Janine piped, "Abbey? I just always imagined a houseful of kids for myself, you know? And a dog and a cat and maybe a canary. A big bay window, a sitting room… I guess I can still try to make that happen."

"You have plenty of time," Bee offered firmly. "That's something I am sure of. And you know what else you have to look forward to?"

Janine's eyes sparkled.

"The Universe throws you little bits of magic sometimes… To make life fun, interesting, to steer you in a new direction, to remind you to wake up, to-" And she stopped abruptly, eyes glazing a little as she drifted in thought.

Janine waited a moment, then called to her, "Bee? You all right?"

Somewhat distantly, Abbey replied. "Yeah. Just... there was something there about reminding myself..." And she inhaled, forcing her gaze back across the table. "Hmm. It'll come back to me, I guess. It's just a little blurry right now.

"Anyway, what I meant to say -and maybe it's connected to that thread of constancy I mentioned before- there are little magical prompts, nudges somehow... So expect those too. Watch for them, they'll help you along. Some people don't ever take time to notice, and it's truly a loss. So watch for the magic. Take notice."

And with that, she rose and grabbed the check, escorting the younger woman to the door.

It happened. Abbey Taft drove out to the Whelton Township Post Office, gingerly pulled the key from her necklace, jiggled it just so in the lock... and opened the box door to find it utterly empty. Her lungs instinctively sucked in a loud gasp of stagnant air... her hand went to her face. Then she caught herself. "Just no mail today," she said aloud, forcing optimism. "My letter to myself, who knows when and where it's being read. But at least it's on its way..."

It struck her how this simple little moment of emptiness felt. Yet instead of dwelling, Abbey made herself speak again: "I'm really glad for the experience of the letters. And the locket. I'm really glad."

She returned the key to her necklace, and drove home. She'd make her way back to Whelton soon enough. And see what happened.

That night, after putting Molly to bed, Abbey poured two glasses of whiskey & soda and sat herself down at the kitchen table. For once in a long, long time, she imagined what it would be like to sit here, with her father… how it would be today, if he were still alive.

"I wonder if you'd have disclosed certain things to me, Daddy," she began, "if I'd been more mature. If I'd been older while you were alive. Or if you were here instead of Mom, maybe you'd have said things you never would have told me before…"

She sipped at her drink; the ice cubes chinked. She pushed the second glass across to where she imagined her father would be joining her tonight, here, at her table.

"Mom married you with a broken heart, didn't she? I bet that was hard on you. Still, it's not all about her. That's only half the story, right?

"Why don't you scream in my dreams, Dad, when the flood comes? Why didn't you write me a letter? Why so much silence?"

She tried to envision her father seated here, leaning in the chair, tilting back a long draw of the whiskey. His hair was longer than usual. His eyes were deeply tired. He faced her. Yet still he said nothing.

"You were a young man… looking forward to the future. You married a beautiful, intelligent girl who had her earliest memories of the farm but then had been uprooted to the city. By the time she was in college and met you, she was city-smart, probably edgy, independent, exciting. But underneath all that, deep underneath, she came to you unhealed; hurting. Maybe she handed that off to you, expected you to help her grieve… but she never actually let you in on it. I could see that maybe she never even told you how sad it was…

"And your bright future got a little bit dimmer, a little overshadowed... Did you resent her? Or did you love her so much you just wanted to knock down the walls and hold her until she screamed it all out... but she never would..." Bee paused, wondering. Slowly, she sipped at her drink, considering whether or not any of her speculations were the least bit accurate. "Did she refuse to ever let you that close, Dad? Was that it?"

And she coaxed him some more; she reminisced, she went over details out loud that she recalled from old photographs, old family tales, past family moments joyful and sad. She remembered her father's voice: the tinge of raspiness at the end of the day, the hint of Midwestern in his drawl. But the spirit of him would say nothing more, not even now.

After sipping the last of her whiskey, Abbey pulled a piece of paper from the kitchen drawer and, without much hesitation, began writing:

Dear Dad,

There's a lot I don't know about you, I'm realizing. I know for certain you never were a coward, so that's not it. And I know you weren't superficial, or uninteresting, so that's not it either. But somehow, in some way, I don't think you lived your potential... otherwise I'd feel like I knew you better. And I have to tell you, Dad, it's a copout. It's some kind of a betrayal.

I can understand when a distrust of intimacy gets seeded, because of fearing another heartbreak. –Mom had that, I know now... but what about you? I'm not blaming either of you, I'm not excusing you either. And I just want to know.

:Did you feel like you lived your life? If not, can you tell me how to avoid doing the same thing? Maybe what I can tell Molly so she avoids it?

I know some days and some years have their emptiness, their lack of clarity, their ongoing disappointments... But isn't there a way to live, to connect, to reach -despite all that??

These are the important lessons, I get that now. And I feel you're trying to tell me something, Dad. You are trying to remind me of a certain direction. But I don't understand; God knows I don't understand it all. I know you didn't either. I never expected you to.

I'll write again soon.

Love from Abbey

On Monday, Abbey spontaneously stayed home from work, called Greta and happily gave her the day off, and packed a picnic for herself and Molly to go visit the zoo. Molly squealed with excitement, reassuring Aspen she'd report back all the details especially about the wolves and prairie dogs. Bee chuckled at the little girl, mussing her hair. "C'mon, Sweetie," she urged, and they made their way to the car.

"Can I get a cotton candy, Mommy?" Molly piped, buckling her seat belt.

"We'll see," Bee told her. "I'm sure we'll get a treat by the end of the day. Wait and see."

Molly squealed again, and began singing a song about animals that she'd learned at preschool. The morning held a chill but was sunny, promising a perfect day.

Molly Taft loved the lemurs -she toted her mother around the exhibit several times, watching the primates swing, play and munch on fruit. She and Abbey also spent a long time watching the elephants saunter along, and the giraffes pull leaves from tall branches.

In the lorikeet house, Molly helped calm an upset two-year-old, who was having trouble keeping still long enough for one of the little parrots to land on her hand. Molly showed her how, and with no prompting from the child's parents, retrieved another bowl of nectar for the girl, to entice a second visit from the hungry bird.

With a grin, Molly then took her mother's hand and pulled her along to find the prairie dogs. "We'll have to take a picture, Mommy," she said. "Aspen will love it! …Hey Mommy, do they call their babies 'prairie puppies'?"

After lunch, Abbey let her daughter pick out a tuft of purple cotton candy, and they wandered further midst the outdoor exhibits. At the end of their visit, they ventured into the petting zoo, where Molly loved spending time up close with the big horn sheep, the llamas, zebra and the camel. Little goats crooned, crowding the child as she handed down feed.

"Their lips tickle!" she giggled, looking up gleefully as Abbey snapped photos.

The two-year-old from earlier entered the pen, and quickly dropped her father's hand to hurry over toward Molly. Bee took a few more pictures, struck by Molly's easy demeanor with the younger child. As the goats ambled away, Molly bent down on her knees to cup the last bits of feed with the toddler. Together, they made bleating noises, calling back the small animals.

The other parents smiled along with Abbey. "Here's my phone number," said the little girl's father. "Text me a copy. Your daughter is adorable, by the way." As they all left the petting zoo, he took time to thank Molly for her helpfulness.

Molly nodded. A little tired and shy, she hung close to her mother's side. "Well, time to go, Molli-pop," Abbey smiled. "Aspen's waiting to hear all about our great day."

Agreeing, the little girl leaned even closer as they headed out to the car.

Leading up to Thanksgiving, Abbey visited Bonaday's quite often. She found that her mother had a renewed interest in cards: they played round after round of King-in-the-Corner, Go-Fish and Rummy. Abbey and Molly visited for supper one night, ordering trays from the cafeteria and eating alongside Caroline, Missy and John-Wyatt, whose daughter Betsy also joined their circle.

Afterward, Bee and Molly sat with Caroline in her room, the t.v. droning game shows. Molly was propped on the bed, nearly dozing. Bee had sparked a new project with her mother -each of the women was fumbling with crochet hooks, attempting colorful scarves and hats for holiday gifts. Caroline watched the television more carefully than her work; nonetheless, Bee enjoyed their time together.

"We've got quite a few done so far, see Mom?" Bee realized, thumbing through the assortment in their basket. "Who do you think this hat is for?"

To her surprise, Caroline answered at once: "Greta."

"Oh? Really?" She hadn't expected such a quick and direct reply; unexpected too was the choice to give a striped green and white knitted hat to her friend. She grinned. "Well, excellent, Mom. Greta will appreciate you thinking of her -I'm sure of that!"

Without hesitation, Caroline continued naming gift recipients, almost too quickly for Abbey to keep up. "Woah," she said. "Do you happen to have any safety pins in here, Mom? We can attach labels; it'll make it easier to remember."

The commercials over, Caroline turned all attention back to the t.v. Abbey sighed a little, but dug through the basket, then stood up to look in the bathroom for pins. With no luck, she pulled at the drawers of the desk, then she happened to glance at the bureau and caught sight of her mother's jewelry box.

Taking a few steps across the room, Bee suddenly wondered if Caroline's own locket would be tucked inside. Gingerly, she pulled open the lid.

The pendants, brooches, strand of pearls, bracelets and rings were perfectly organized. Bee hadn't seen these treasures in awhile, but she recognized nearly every one. There was no locket. "No safety pins either," she muttered aloud, just about to shut the box. Then her hand was drawn to the bottom of the case, where an ornate and somewhat discolored kerchief lay tucked beneath the necklaces. Its lacy corner was visible, with a monogram partially folded under. Bee carefully fingered it free: C C T. Her mother's initials. To see them was comforting -in recent years it seemed so often that Caroline's personality was slipping away… This simple keepsake somehow reaffirmed her identity.

Abbey smiled softly, stroking the kerchief. A little hint of roughness caught her attention. A paper was underneath, hidden there. She gasped.

With care, she moved the necklaces and then pulled at the embroidered kerchief. Below, just there, was a folded piece of paper, yellowed with time.

Abbey turned to her mother, who was still fascinated by the television, her lips moving almost unnoticeably as she mumbled answers in response to the game show host.

Bee sat at the edge of the bed. Molly, by now, was fast asleep. Taking a breath, Abbey delicately unfolded the paper, feeling her anticipation rise just as if she were back at the post office.

Yes.

This was from her father.

Chapter Eighteen

Bee had waited until the television program was over before she called across the room to her mother. But even then, with the t.v. turned off, Caroline didn't offer any words in reply to Abbey's questions. She didn't say anything at all after her daughter read the few sentences scrawled on the page in her hand.

"Do you remember Dad?" Bee asked, a little impatient, after the long stretch of silence. "Do you remember your husband, Caroline? His name was Donald. Donald Taft." And she pulled a photo frame from the nightstand, holding it up.

Caroline watched, but she did not respond.

Then Abbey softened, and set the photo down. "Donald was a good husband. You married a good, kind man." She paused, gazing to her mother. Then she said, "Donald, he wrote you a letter. Let me read it again…"

Dear Caroline Claire,

Happy Valentines Day.

I will miss you and the kids while I'm away

on business this week. I hope maybe we can

go to the lake again later this month when

I'm back home - what do you think?

I'll bring you a little something from Toronto.

Remember that I love you. -Donald

When Abbey saw Greta the next day, she explained how her mother never did respond to the words of the letter, other than the fact that she watched closely as Bee read it twice through and she paid attention as her daughter returned it gently to its place in the jewelry box.

Bee went on to tell Greta how she'd then curled up on the bed alongside Molly, and without realizing it, had fallen fast asleep. The morning arrived quickly -Bee had been so deeply asleep she hadn't even turned over. When she wakened, her mother was already up and dressed, readying for breakfast. "Omelet Thursday and fresh biscuits for soakies," she had called to the two in her bed, as she tugged on the doorknob to make her way to the community room.

Abbey had giggled, watching her go. Then she rolled back to Molly and hugged her close. Something pinched below her chin as she squeezed the little girl. Adjusting and halfway sitting up, Abbey reached and realized there was a second gold strand now about her neck, intertwined with the one on which she kept her Whelton key. A second strand… Her mother had returned the locket.

Greta wasn't surprised. "It was meant for you," she said plainly, smile widening. "And your mom knows it. Somehow, some way. Abbey, you're reaching her."

"She's reaching back," Bee nodded. And she ran her fingers over the circle of the locket once more.

"It's amazing to me, Greta," she said, "how out of all the cards and letters Dad must have written over the years, this was the one she saved. This was the one that gets passed down. It's so bizarre, these little mismatched tidbits and clues of our lives, that somehow transcend time... It seems so random."

Greta only nodded.

"And it's like they're all fashioned together -some weird invisible thread- that spans backward into the past and forward into the future..." The gaze she offered to her friend sparked with a particular urgency. "What is that? What is that mechanism? What is it called??"

Greta smiled tenderly, holding Abbey's stare, taking a long breath to fill the silence. "I don't know what it's called," she finally said. "But it's set into motion through intimacy, through connection. Through love. Maybe not necessarily romantic love or even what we define as platonic love, or the love that translates into happiness, or even that kind of Hollywood love that can be whittled down into soundbytes… It's the kind of interconnection that's the foundation underneath all that. Primal, somehow. Holy, maybe. And it just cycles 'round, infinitely, that's why it seems timeless."

"How the hell do you have all these answers?" Bee put to her, expression abruptly more pointed and much less serious.

They laughed together, a little forced, but it served to temper the moment. Abbey commented on it. "The vastness to all this, it can be a little dizzying," she said.

Greta agreed, not missing a beat. After a brief pause she took her voice to a whisper: "Some people never even notice it... And others, we yearn for it. We can't live without it."

This time Bee nodded. "It's quite a phenomenon..." she uttered, and let her stare drift away toward the window.

Abbey's sister Kate was always eager to send out Christmas cards early. She gathered her kids just after Halloween and all together they drew and colored a holiday picture to create a signature family card. Over the years, the complexity of the drawings had evolved; it was always a treat when they arrived. By now even young Molly knew to look for the monogrammed red envelopes sometime in late November -when it arrived this year she tore open the seal all by herself.

"Look, Mommy!" she called across the house. "Bryn and Taylor drew Santa's sleigh. Look at the reindeers!" She found Abbey in the living room and shook the card excitedly. Together they counted out the deer and decided which one was Rudolph.

As the little girl scampered away, Bee checked the envelope for a letter.

She found a short note and a thick fold of papers. Without reading, she curiously unfolded the white square of pages. They were copies Kate had made: the first was Caroline's birth certificate.

    Caroline Claire Elbertson

    Born December 4, 1935

    Logansport, IN

    Parents Adam B. Elbertson

    and Maggie Clarke Elbertson

    Time of Birth: 7:59AM

    Weight: 5lbs. 12oz.

Abbey ran her fingers over the old inked footprint. It was so tiny, and struck her as odd to think of her mother as the new little baby she once was. It brought her to a smile.

Then she tugged at the second paper -this too was a birth certificate. Abbey's smile broadened to see it, though this one was tinged with sadness as well:

    Hannah Claire Elbertson

    Born December 4, 1935

    Logansport, IN

    Parents Adam B. Elbertson

    and Maggie Clarke Elbertson

    Time of Birth: 8:16 AM

    Weight: 5lbs. 4oz.

"Precious," Bee said aloud, now touching the footprint of her aunt. "So precious."

She stared at the papers a long while, then thought of Kate.

"Incredible," she added, and picked up the phone to call her sister.

John Jaffers was bright-eyed tonight. He waved across the room in a wide motion. Beside him, Greta too beamed happily. They were both excited to see Abbey round the corner and join them at the table for dinner.

"So proud of you!" John triumphed, smacking a kiss on her cheek as Bee sat down.

She exaggerated an exhalation. "Whew!"

"One of America's Top Women's Magazines!" he exclaimed, toasting with a glass of wine and slapping the newspaper in front of Abbey. "Congrats, Ms. Editor. You continue to reach new heights."

"Well thank you, thank you, My Friends," she said, chuckling. "It is a little unexpected. But everybody at the office is ecstatic, that's for sure."

John winked to her. Greta added, "Well I'm especially proud of you for trusting another babysitter and inviting me out with the big kids," she quipped, sipping at the wine.

"Here, here," John agreed, raising his glass once again. "Now let's get down to some serious drinking. Ladies?"

The three enjoyed themselves, ordered bruschetta and a cheese sampler, exchanged stories of recent weeks. John and his wife were planning to spend the holidays in London. Abbey teased him a bit: "Why not a trip to the Grand Canyon? -Or Miami? -Or Idaho? It's beautiful there in winter…"

John scoffed. "Simply put, my Dear -it's not far enough away from the office and the in-laws."

Abbey rolled her eyes, well aware he was kidding.

"Of course the main reason is low airfare right now," he added, winking again. "And we do delight in a spot of proper tea. And Susan loves Europe -she's always wanted to be in London at Christmastime."

"Ahh, that's better then," Bee said, giving him a more familiar smile. Then she turned to Greta expectantly.

"Mmm, my vacation won't be quite as romantic," the woman said, nibbling a square of parmesan. "But I look forward to it. As you know, most of my family is outside D.C. We'll all be together down there for the week."

There was a moment's pause then John asked, "Hey Bee, any more letters recently? I've been meaning to ask."

"No…" She and Greta exchanged comments on the cheese samples. Then she caught herself, "Oh, actually, there was a new letter the other day. I found it unexpectedly in Mom's things at Bonaday's…" And her eyes sparkled. "It was finally from my Dad."

John was immediately intrigued. Abbey shared more, "You know, I've been thinking a lot lately how much Dad wasn't as present back when I was younger. Well, in certain ways…" She added, "Anyway, this

190

letter was refreshing. It was sweet to hear from him, see his handwriting, read the words he chose. You know?"

John nodded in understanding. "Anything as personal as a letter from my father would be amazing," he said. "You're lucky, Bee."

"Yes," she agreed. "All of this has been bizarre... hard... surreal... but yes, I know that I'm lucky."

Again there was a pause. John poured more wine, Abbey and Greta chased after the last square of nutty parmesan. As Greta raised her fork, victorious, Abbey sat back and watched her friends for a long uninterrupted moment. Then she cleared her throat and said, "I have a little announcement..."

John and Greta gave her full attention, discerning the hint of a tremble in her voice.

"I'm -I'm going to visit an adoption agency over the holidays." It was obvious that saying the words aloud made the decision that much more real for Abbey.

Without hesitation, Greta reached to embrace her and John whooped a cheer. "Oh my God, Sweetie, how long have you been keeping this little morsel from us?" He too gave her a joyful hug.

"Well," she told them, "it's been just sort-of occurring to me for some time... The locket really led me to the realization, I think... or maybe not. I'm not sure." And she smiled sweetly. "I mean I thought about it, years ago, that I'd like Molly to have a sibling... but things weren't quite in place." And she cleared her throat again, steadying. "But it's become more obvious to me that someone is missing: My second child is missing. And I know," she added, her eyes gleaming, "that Hannah helped all this along…"

Greta reached for her again.

"Is that spooky?" Abbey asked her. "Am I just trying to fill some long-lost void in the family?"

"Sh, sh," Greta reassured her. "You deserve your own complete family, Bee. Just the way you want it. And of course the past helps point to our future. And of course we do what we can to heal old wounds. But you wouldn't want another baby just for that reason.

"So no, it isn't spooky. It's wonderful. It's wonderful."

John reassured her as well, his arm around her, squeezing tight. "Today's modern woman, so many decisions to make…" he teased, lightening the moment. "It's not as simple as going to bed with the hubby and waking up preggers, is it?"

Abbey swatted at him. Then she added, "No. No it's not that simple. And yes, it can all be overwhelming sometimes."

Greta tugged at her arm. "Listen, Bee, if part of what this has been about -the key, the letters, the locket- is bringing you to your baby, that's a beautiful, beautiful thing. It makes sense," and she gripped Abbey's hand. "It's been about reaffirming your family, that's a beautiful thing." She smiled. "It's been about you. As a daughter, as a sister, as a friend, as a mother. Congratulations."

"Thank you so much, Greta," Bee said to her. And she gazed across the table, watching the expectation and happiness in her friends' warm expressions. "Wow…" she uttered. "I'm going to have a baby… I really am. Wow."

"Job security for you," John pointed out, nudging at Greta. They all chuckled.

With a stretch, the man happened to glance about the restaurant. "Oh," he said, "what a coincidence. Isn't that the dashing Mr. Cole up at the bar?"

The women turned. "He's drinking alone?" Greta asked, a little quizzical.

"Mm," Bee nodded, flipping open a menu. "I've heard through the grapevine he's single again…" She seemed a little disinterested.

Greta and John exchanged a look, then both reached to pull the menu away from her. "Go," John mouthed. Greta agreed.

Abbey raised a brow.

"You were going to ask him out a few months ago."

John turned in his seat again, to get a better look. "Abbey Elana, he's gorgeous. Go, my Dear. Tell him you're having his baby…"

Bee swatted him even harder this time. Then she stood, but eyed Greta: "I thought we decided this 'truelove' thing wasn't about the romantic…"

"It's a bonus," the woman offered emphatically, raising a thumb and gesturing once again to the bar.

Abbey shrugged her shoulders, a little uncertain, and made her way across the room.

The next Saturday, Abbey and Molly Taft took a drive. It turned out to be a full morning's adventure, as they made their way well past Whelton before spotting the sign they were looking for: "Estate Sale" in broad letters, with an arrow pointing the new direction.

Molly dashed past the furniture to the strands of long beads of necklaces and fine scarves; Abbey picked more carefully through the array of special keepsakes, the lines of antiques, the assortment of everyday belongings.

She touched some of the items fondly, knowing well each was sacred, and Catherine came to mind. Indeed, Bee thought, she needed to thank that woman again… if for no other reason than the renewed anticipation she felt now at the start of each day. There was sustenance in that momentum; it was beyond measure.

Molly came close and tugged her mother's hand. "Can I get these?" she piped, holding up a strand of crystal beads and a silvered pocketbook. A little compact mirror was inside, that clicked when Molly popped it open.

"Of course," Bee told the little girl. "That's why we're here, right?"

"This too?" Molly asked, meekly, raising a tiny framed watercolor. It was a rendering of a sandcastle, hand-painted by someone long ago. "For my brother or sister?"

Bee could only smile wide to the child, and reach to pat her cheek.

Molly beamed, hopping alongside as they made their way into the sitting room. As they rounded the corner, a shadow criss-crossed over a rocking chair against the far wall. Catching a quick glimpse, for a moment Abbey was sure it was her father. "Treasures all, Dad," she whispered, gazing across the empty room. "Treasures all." And she took her daughter's hand once more, wandering through the open doorway toward the new discoveries that called them forward.

_____

Mom,

I wanted to write to you. There's a lot to say; a lot I'd like to say right now. But I think the heart of it is this -unexpected things happen in Life. I know that now like never before... Things that jar us. We feel betrayed by Fate... betrayed by those around us who leave; those who find happiness; those who disappear one way or another. Maybe Hannah haunted you. Maybe your parents were so heartbroken too that they couldn't talk about her enough while you were growing up. Maybe the move from the farm was, for them, an escape... but for you, just another heartbreak...

And I don't know if there were other terrible losses in your life... Maybe Dad did something, maybe I did... Maybe we didn't do something we should have... I don't know those details. But I do know that there are tragedies. Midst all of Life's wonder and triumphs, there are indeed those sad and horrible moments. And I realize that now about you and your life, and about everyone else's too.

That understanding, for me, has become a gift. It's gotten me beyond myself. And I thank you for that.

I'm sure some philosopher said it better than I can, but... 'It's not the tragedies or the injustices or the challenges in Life that define us; it's how we choose to learn from them and keep loving and connecting afterward, and onward into the days and years that come. It is indeed that outlook we keep for ourselves, that we maintain, even in the hardest times, even after the hardships try to steal it away.'

This is what you've taught me, Mom. I've had other teachers along the way, but maybe they were just re-emphasizing to help get it through to me. Well, this is one of the big lessons that I've finally taken in. This is the key you've passed down to me, and to Molly. -Not the emptiness, not the something-missing, not the grief... but the realization that there is growth, and maybe even new hope, despite that.

I thank you for it, Mom. And I thank Dad too, for his part. I may not always have been an easy student, I'm sure, but thanks for not giving up on me.

And I know there are still things left between us, still things for us to work out and try to understand about each other. That's natural; an unending story -the way it should be.

But what's important right now is for you to know -for both of us to know- that I treasure what you've given; I treasure who you are; I treasure our connection. It's timeless.

I love you, Mom.

Love from Abbey

———————————————

In memory of~

Beatrice DeVoid Preston, my grandmother, whose 1915 locket inspired part of this story, and the title & cover of this book.

With loving thoughts of my Aunt Clariann;

And for my Aunt Elaine, Uncle John, Onkel Hans, Cousin Elfrieda, Aunt Betty & her daughter, and for the others too, unnamed or unknown, who for too brief a time had their place as the firstborn in our family.

Please visit the author's website for additional works,
contact information & links to social media:

www.MariannePuechl.com